Beyond Tradition

SEVEN REIMAGINED TALES FROM JAPAN

CLAIRE E. HALLINAN

ISBN: 978-1-7330356-7-5

Dedication

For Marysue and Joel,

the inspiration of behind Reimagined Urashima

Preface

Dear Reader,

If you consider yourself a devoted aficionado of Japanese culture, you are already acquainted with the captivating narratives that lie ahead. If you are not, no worries! Every native Japanese individual grows up immersed in the beloved folktales of Momotaro and Urashima Taro. While numerous books have been published, presenting standardized storylines, it is important to note that these tales were initially passed down orally through generations. Consequently, certain details may exhibit slight variations depending on the perspectives of publishers and authors. Yet, the allure of Japanese folktales for enthusiasts lies in their enchanting and distinctive magical sequences, set within cultural landscapes adorned with secluded islands embraced by mountains and sea. Delving into these enthralling, unpredictable, and mystical episodes grants readers a myriad of pleasurable and diverse experiences. While folktales from around the world possess inherent creativity, Japanese folklore distinguishes itself through its traditions, climates, and customs. Thus, when immersing yourself in Japanese folktales, you not only find entertainment but also gain insight into Japanese culture.

Allow me to highlight a few intriguing aspects of the Japanese folktales I have chosen. First and foremost, many of these tales commence with a childless elderly couple. These diligent and affectionate partners, burdened by the absence of both offspring and wealth, experience a wondrous discovery through extraordinary means. Their child, blessed with extraordinary abilities, ultimately brings joy to their aged hearts—though, as with any tale, exceptions do exist. In those instances not centered around newborn infants, certain characters exhibit astonishing yet endearing superstitious tendencies.

While most Japanese folktales culminate in happiness, a few exceptions, such as Urashima Taro and Kaguya Hime, conclude on a sorrowful note—unlike the majority of their counterparts. Curiously enough, these melancholic endings revolve around the themes of aging and empty nests. It is ironic that such tales interweave the realities of life into their fabric, evoking sadness. Often, we dismiss these important aspects, despite their inescapability, merely out of fear.

As readers, we yearn for blissful resolutions above all else. In my rendition of Japanese folktales, I aspire to prompt contemplation about embracing life's events, just as the characters within each story do. Aging and experiencing the empty nest syndrome are natural and gradual processes that involve a sense of grief. However, I believe it's crucial for individuals to learn how to embrace and cope with these realities, in order to continue their own life journey. Essentially, I wanted all of my favorite characters to live their stories to the fullest with my unique twists.

In this book, every chapter embodies a carefully chosen symbolic element from Japanese folktale. Following each tale, I delve into my imagination, weaving together a tapestry that spans from rice balls to sci-fi elements to profound reverence. Within these folktales, seemingly ordinary items or events undergo a magnificent transformation, becoming imbued with magic and extraordinary qualities. What adds to their fascination is the unique collision between what used to be seen as normal scenes from many decades ago and the present time, making the tale significant and meaningful.

It is my delight as an author to skillfully navigate the narratives, using the stories as a playground to captivate and entertain rea ders.Whenever I revisit these cherished tales from my childhood, whether by perusing them silently, reciting them aloud, or listening to others read, a wave of nostalgia envelops me. It transports me back to the very bed where my grandmother spun her yarns, or to the warmth of my mother's embrace, where my siblings and I vied for prime positions during her storytelling sessions.

Now, it is my turn to pass on these tales to the next generation, adding my own unique twists. Infusing traditional stories with a blend of modern Japanese and the United States' cultures was merely the inception of this endeavor. By weaving my inner experiences—both the sorrows and the hopes—into Japanese folktales, I aim to provide you with a distinct form of entertainment. Narrating a familiar story through the prism of my creativity brings me pure joy. Sharing my rendition of

Japanese folktales is an honor, and I humbly express my gratitude for your decision to embark upon this one-of-a-kind adventure.

I sincerely hope that you relish every page of my creative adaptation, spanning from cover to cover.

Your favorite author,

Claire E. Hallinan

Dear Japanese Readers:
日本人読者の皆さんへ

日本の公立学校では英語は必須科目となっていますが、ネイティブを目の前にしてコミュニケーションできるか、ときかれると、それはちょっと、となりますよね。私もそうでした。でも洋書をすらすらと読んでいる人を見ると羨ましくって、私もあんな風に読めるようになりたいな、とずっと夢見ていました。

アメリカの小学校では、英語を読む能力が低くても、自分に興味のある話題の本ならば多少レベルが高くても読む努力をし、理解し、結果、読書を楽しむことができるという事実事実が毎日実践実証されています。学校図書館の検索にも興味のあるカテゴリーを入力してお気に入りの本を探すと、読書の意欲が増えてきます。

日本でも、英語に強くなりたいが、洋書を読むのはまだ自信がないというという人でも、もし興味のある内容だったり、よく知っている物語だったりすると、読みたくなるし、ちょっとつまづいてもすぐに挫折することはないはずです。日本人なら誰もがよく知っている物語といえば、日本昔話。日本昔話を今風にアレンジすることによって難しすぎるというレベルから、これくらいなら私でもわかる、というレベルで英語を楽しんで読む経験ができることと思います。

取り上げた昔話は私の祖母から小さいころ毎日のように聞いたもの、母が読み聞かせてくれたものなど色々ですがアレンジするにあたっては私の個人的な人生経験エピソードや現在の気になる社会現象を織り込んでみました。

参考、引用した昔話
ももたろう Peach Boy
うぐいすひめ Warbler Princess
うらしまたろう Urashima
かぐや姫 Princess Kaguya
かさじぞう Statues with Straw Hats
金たろう Power Boy
さるかに合戦　Monkey vs. Crabs
ないた赤おに Crying Demon

表表紙から裏表紙の隅々まで読んでいただけるとこんな幸いなことはありません。
クレア英津子ハリナン

Contents

1

Wholesome Rice Balls

THE FRAGRANCE OF RICE EXCEEDS THE FRAGRANCE OF FLOWERS. ~JAPANESE PROVERB

***Omusubi Kororin* Rolling Rice Balls**

Once upon a time, in a small village nestled in Northern Japan, lived Ojii-san (Old Man) and Obaa-san (Old Woman). Their village was renowned for its exceptional rice production, thanks to the pristine waters that flowed from the melted winter snow. Ojii-san and Obaa-san, like most villagers, dedicated themselves to rice farming and worked tirelessly in the fields day after day. And for every lunchtime excursion to the rice fields, Obaa-san would diligently prepare fist-sized rice balls, while Ojii-san lent a hand in the kitchen by expertly wrapping them with seaweed.

Alongside their rice farming endeavors, Ojii-san had another peculiar occupation, one that supported their family's livelihood. From the warm spring days to the breathtaking autumn scenes, he ventured into the neighboring hills, collecting tree branches to sell. These branches were perfect kindling for campfires, and each day, Ojii-san filled his backpack with them. It may have seemed like a simple task, but for Ojii-san, it went beyond merely picking branches. He took great care in planting new trees in barren areas, ensuring the continued growth of a thriving forest ecosystem. His dedication extended to meticulously calculating the distance between each tree, monitoring their growth rates, and conducting research to promote a healthy and balanced environment. Yes, he was a rice farmer and a logger, but he was also a self-made forestry biologist and a passionate environmentalist.

One day, the sun reached its peak in the sky and cast a warm glow over the land, Ojii-san realized it was time for his midday meal. He lowered himself gently onto his favorite spot, settling down comfortably. Excitedly, he grabbed his lunchbox and gently placed it on his lap. He slowly opened it, eager to take the first delicious bite of his homemade rice ball. However, right before he could enjoy that mouthwatering morsel, an annoyingly busy fly zoomed back and forth around Ojii-san's rice ball, ruining his peaceful moment. Irritated, he moved to swat away the annoying bug, but instead knocked one of his precious rice balls out of the lunchbox.

The rice ball went tumbling down the hill, and poor Ojii-san started panicking. "Wait! My rice ball!" he cried out desperately. Holding his lunchbox tightly, he watched in distress as the rice ball picked up speed, rolling farther away from him. Even though the loss of one rice ball may not seem like a big deal, it meant the world to Ojii-san. That single rice ball represented his hard work in the fields, the essence of a successful harvest, and Obaa-san's loving effort in making the delicious treat. Determined not to let it escape, he carefully made his way down the hill, following the path of the mischievous rice ball.

As Ojii-san approached the bottom of the hill, he was delighted to hear a gentle and enchanting melody floating in the air. With piqued curiosity, he followed the melodic tunes, which led him to a small hole that resembled an animal's burrow. It became evident that his rice ball had managed to find its way into this intriguing opening. The captivating song continued to play, with lyrics echoing, "Rolling, falling from the sky. Eat, feast, dance, and pounce!"

As the music faded to silence, Ojii-san devised a plan. "Maybe if I offer another rice ball, the festivities will continue," he pondered. With no hesitation, he fetched a second rice ball and dropped it into the hole. Instantly, the joyful melody resurfaced, even more vibrant and spirited than before. Ojii-san, moved by the infectious energy, found himself dancing along. The voices from the hole, though disembodied, joined in and cheerfully exclaimed, "Rolling, falling from the sky. Eat, feast, dance, and pounce! Is that you, Ojii-san? You rock'n rice ball!"

Caught up in the joyous celebration, Ojii-san couldn't resist the temptation to drop his final rice ball into the hole. Like an addict chasing a high, he yearned to bask in the lively atmosphere and listen to the cheerful, friendly song that lifted his spirits. With a triumphant "pop," the music started once more. Overwhelmed with happiness, Ojii-san sang along, "Rolling, falling from the sky. Eat, feast, dance, and pounce." The voices from the hole warmly invited him to join their party. Without a moment's hesitation, he leaped into the hole, eager to embrace the festivities.

As Ojii-san descended, a rush of fear overcame him, and he couldn't help but scream in dismay. The hole turned out to be much deeper than he expected, and he tumbled and twirled, his senses overwhelmed. Finally, with a loud thud, he landed on solid ground. To his astonishment, he found himself surrounded by a gathering of mice, all dressed in fancy outfits. They greeted him with gratitude, expressing their heartfelt appreciation for the delicious rice balls he had shared. Ojii-san was captivated by the scene unfolding before him—strong little mice taking turns pounding mochi rice with miniature pestles and mortars, while a mouthwatering and colorful feast filled the air with enticing aromas. It felt as if the New Year had arrived right there in front of him.

Completely enchanted by the magical moment, Ojii-san couldn't contain his excitement and exclaimed, "Oh my goodness, it feels like a dream come true!" One of the friendly mice approached him politely and said, "Ojii-san, we are truly grateful for your rice balls! This is our way of expressing our thanks. Please enjoy our celebration." With that, she poured a sake drink into his cup, and the singers resumed their melodies, while the dancers gracefully swayed to the music.

It was a magnificent feast and an extraordinary spectacle created especially for Ojii-san. He delighted in the delicacies and the mice's captivating performances, fully immersing himself in the jubilant celebration. Time seemed to slip away unnoticed, as he embraced every moment of joy.

After many hours, a mouse dressed in a beautiful kimono picked up a koto, a traditional Japanese string instrument, and started to play. The melody transported Ojii-san back in time—he remembered the day he first met Obaa-san on a stunning beach, so many decades ago. As he soaked in the nostalgic atmosphere, reality hit him like a slap in the face. “Oh no! Obaa-san must be so worried about me. I need to head back home!” Ojii-san quickly let the mice know about his urgent departure. Thankfully, they understood his situation and gave him a parting gift, a lovely omiyage souvenir. Grateful beyond words, Ojii-san thanked them from the bottom of his heart, assuring them that Obaa-san would be absolutely thrilled by their thoughtfulness.

No sooner had the mouse finished talking than Ojii-san found himself back in his usual surroundings, the place where he had initially set out to enjoy his lunch. However, instead of his regular lunchbox, he now held a beautifully decorated box—the souvenir given to him by the mice. “Am I in a dream?” he pondered, feeling completely bewildered. With the sun beginning to set, Ojii-san hurried back home.

“I’m back, Obaa-san!” he cheerfully called out, sliding open the entrance door. To his surprise, he found himself surrounded by all the familiar objects and furniture, but Obaa-san was nowhere to be seen. As he made his way toward the family altar, a sense of unease washed over him. There, he discovered a picture of himself, leaving him utterly puzzled. “What’s happening? How long have I been away?” Suddenly, the entrance door creaked open, and a little white dog came bounding toward him, growling fiercely. “Rrrrr, ruff, ruff, ruff, rrr.” It seemed that the dog viewed him with suspicion. Obaa-san had found the dog, Pochi, in the local animal shelter after Ojii-san’s disappearance. Pochi had become the perfect furry companion and protector to help Obaa-san heal her pain from losing Ojii-san. Pochi was obedient, fun, and best of all, he helped Obaa-san forget about the desperate loneliness. Obaa-san stepped into the room and calmed her beloved companion, "Take it easy, Pochi. What's happening here?" Then she stood frozen in astonishment. "O-O-Ojii-san? Are you a ghost?" she stammered, her eyes filled with disbelief.

"What are you talking about? It's me! I'm finally home!" Ojii-san reassured her, trying to ease her confusion. However, Obaa-san, struggling to understand the situation, shared that Ojii-san had vanished from his work seven long years ago, leaving her in a constant state of worry. "Seven years? That can't be! I had the most incredible time at the mice's party!" Ojii-san exclaimed. The disbelief was heavy in the air as they tried to make sense of the extraordinary events that had unfolded. Despite the challenges of comprehending it all, they celebrated their long-awaited reunion with overwhelming joy. Even Pochi, Obaa-san's loyal companion, quickly adjusted to Ojii-san's return, wagging his tail happily. Ojii-san excitedly showed them the vibrantly colored box the mice had given him, exclaiming, "This is the omiyage souvenir. I wonder what's inside." Obaa-san suggested they should wait until the next morning to open it, considering the late hour and Ojii-san's exhaustion.

Understanding the wisdom in Obaa-san's words, Ojii-san nodded in agreement and replied, "You're absolutely right. I'm completely exhausted. I'll head to bed now. Good night, Obaa-san." With that, he retired to his bedroom, leaving Obaa-san contemplating the contents of the intriguing box. Despite being the one who had suggested waiting, Obaa-san's curiosity became irresistible. Once she heard Ojii-san's familiar snoring through the traditional *shoji* door (paper and wooden sliding door), she tiptoed into the kitchen where Ojii-san had put the box. Gently reaching for the box on top of the cupboard, she placed it on the table and settled down in front of it, offering up mumbled justifications for her actions. "Ojii-san had such a fantastic time because of those rice balls. And who was it that made those rice balls? I think I have every right to open this *omiyage* souvenir box."

With trembling hands, Obaa-san carefully untied the string that encircled the wooden box and lifted the lid with anticipation. To her astonishment, an enormous cloud of white smoke billowed out, immersing her in a flash. Startled and perplexed, she wondered, "What's happening? Is there something else inside?" As she attempted to peer deeper into the box, a powerful force suddenly pulled her entire body toward the box, as if being sucked in by a vacuum cleaner. "Ahhhhhhh!" Everything unfolded so swiftly during her moment of curiosity. Only Pochi, her steady companion, had witnessed the entire sequence of events, including Obaa-san's sudden disappearance. Sadly, no one else would understand what Pochi had seen. The faithful dog sat patiently next to the *omiyage* wooden gift box, longing for her return, hoping for another loving head scratch. But the house was eerily quiet and Obaa-san was nowhere to be found. With a heavy heart, Pochi eventually settled down next to the box and drifted into a deep slumber, filled with hope for Obaa-san's safe return.

Days stretched into weeks, and weeks melted into months. Ojii-san and Pochi shared a deep sense of longing, their hearts filled with melancholy as they dearly missed Obaa-san's presence in their lives. Ojii-san carried the weight of guilt, blaming himself for unintentionally causing Obaa-san's disappearance. Every day, he tirelessly searched for any hint or trace that could bring her back home. Pochi, ever loyal, stood guard by the omiyage wooden box, never wavering in his hope for her return.

One sunny morning, as Ojii-san tended to his modest rice field, a peculiar sight caught his attention. Sprouting from the fertile mud were tiny rice plants before the planting season. Ojii-san's heart skipped a beat, for he recognized these mysterious rice plants as a gift from the magical realm he had once visited. They were a reminder of the extraordinary journey he had undertaken.

As the seasons passed, the rice plants grew tall and strong, swaying gently in the breeze. Ojii-san watched with anticipation, knowing that the bountiful harvest would soon be ready. Each day, he worked tirelessly in the fields, carefully tending to the rice plants and nurturing them with his unwavering dedication.

Finally, the day arrived when the golden rice stalks bowed under the weight of the ripe grains. Ojii-san, filled with a mixture of pride and gratitude, gathered the abundant harvest. The rice grain was plump and glistened like pearls, a testament to Ojii-san's steadfast commitment and the magic that had become a part of his life.

In the harvest celebration, Ojii-san and Pochi hosted a joyous gathering, inviting friends and neighbors from the village. The aroma of freshly cooked rice filled the air, reminding them of Obaa-san's presence. Ojii-san, wearing a warm smile, served the rice to each guest, sharing the fruits of his labor and the magic that had woven through their lives.

As the evening descended and the laughter and chatter filled the air, Ojii-san looked around at the faces of his loved ones, feeling a profound sense of contentment. Suddenly, a familiar sound reached Ojii-san's ears. Soft, melodic music filled the air, reminiscent of the festive tunes he had heard during the mice party in the magical realm. He turned his gaze towards a nearby tree and saw a group of mice, elegantly dressed, carrying trays filled with colorful mochi and rice balls.

The mice, having heard of the bountiful harvest and the joyous gathering, joined in the celebration. Ojii-san's heart swelled with happiness as he watched the mice scampering around, spreading cheer and delight among the guests. They danced and sang, their tiny voices harmonizing with the laughter and conversation of the humans.

Pochi, always a friend to the mice, wagged his tail with excitement and joined in the festivities. The mice offered him small bites of mochi and rice balls, which he happily accepted, savoring the delectable flavors. It was a moment of pure enchantment, where the boundaries between the magical realm and the human world seemed to blur.

From that day forward, Ojii-san and Pochi continued to live out their days, tending to the rice fields with unwavering dedication and savoring the simple joys of life. The mice would occasionally visit, bringing with them their lively presence and delightful treats. The village came to know them as the "Party Mice," and their visits became a cherished tradition, adding an extra sprinkle of magic to Ojii-san and Pochi's lives.

Every day, Ojii-san and Pochi happily went around collecting tree branches, fueled by Ojii-san's firm determination to find that sneaky hole where the rice balls had vanished. They searched high and low, but no matter how much they looked, that teleporting hole seemed to play a never-ending game of hide-and-seek. But you know what? Ojii-san and Pochi weren't keen to throw in the towel. With a sense of curiosity and adventure, Ojii-san and Pochi continued searching, understanding that some things in life are meant to remain a mystery.

And really, where did Obaa-san go? You won't believe where she ended up! Shhhh! Don't tell anyone! It turned out, when Obaa-san opened the souvenir box, a magical smoke whisked her away straight to the mice's den! Can you imagine? Time flew by for her even faster than it did for Ojii-san. She was swept up in all the wild parties with those famous Party Mice. It was likely that this would continue until something triggered her memory of her beloved spouse's or Pochi's presence.

Medetashi, medetashi. Happily Ever After.

2

Magnificent Cherry Blossoms

SCATTERED CHERRY BLOSSOMS, EVEN
THE REMAINING CHERRY BLOSSOMS,
ALSO SCATTERED CHERRY BLOSSOMS.
~RYOKAN OSHO

Hanasaka Jii-san Blooming Old Man

Once upon a time, Ojii-san, an old man, lived with his beloved dog, Pochi. But Pochi had not always been Ojii-san's companion. In fact, it was Ojii-san's wife, Obaa-san, who had found Pochi at the shelter during Ojii-san's seven-year long mysterious disappearance. Upon his return, Obaa-san learned that, while out working in the woods, Ojii-san had chased a rice ball that accidentally fell from his hand and rolled into a mysterious hole. Ojii-san fell into the hole and encountered cheerful music and delicious food—it was a party being held by mice! The endless cuisine and smooth liquor made Ojii-san completely lose track of time. It took seven long years for Ojii-san to finally get home. The night after their dramatic reunion, Obaa-san disappeared in a puff of mysterious smoke right in front of Pochi while Ojii-san was deep asleep.

Since Obaa-san's disappearance, Pochi and Ojii-san grew closer each day, becoming inseparable partners like two peas in a pod. Obaa-san's mysterious departure left Ojii-san feeling haunted, but Pochi was there to lift his spirits with his eager affection and loyal obedience. When Ojii-san was feeling down, Pochi would cheer him up by showering him with sloppy licks on his face, wagging his tail excitedly, begging to play fetch with a tree branch outside, and snuggling up with him on cold, stormy nights. Perhaps, Pochi was missing Obaa-san, too.

As time passed, Ojii-san and Pochi grew older together. However, as you may know, dogs age faster than humans. Ojii-san instinctively sensed that Pochi's final moments were approaching. Day by day, Pochi's movements slowed. He slept longer and his appetite diminished. "Pochi, how are you today? You are the greatest gift I have ever received in my life," Ojii-san whispered, gratefully stroking Pochi's still-rich coat. Pochi quietly responded by resting his chin on Ojii-san's lap.

The next morning, Ojii-san discovered that Pochi was no longer breathing. Tears streamed down from Ojii-san's eyes. He embraced the moment of grief, a moment that encompassed all of his love, gratitude, and longing. "Pochi, thank you for being with me for such a long time.

You will find yourself in a good place," Ojii-san whispered, wiping away his tears.

Pochi was laid to rest in Ojii-san's garden with great respect. His body was gently cremated and given a peaceful burial. The Party Mice, Ojii-san's cherished companions since that unforgettable day of his very first rice ball party, came together in support of Pochi's memorial. They contributed to the ceremonial concessions by offering comforting mochi and rice balls. As the gathering took place, something truly extraordinary unfolded. Right at the spot where Pochi's ashes were buried, a tiny green sprout emerged from the earth. The mice, dressed in their finest attire, stood in utter amazement, scurrying around as if partaking in a sacred dance. Amidst the commotion, the sprout continued to grow rapidly, defying all rules of nature. Ojii-san stood there, speechless and awestruck, his mouth hanging open in disbelief.

The sprout flourished into a magnificent tree, boasting a sturdy trunk. Its branches reached out in every direction. A wide grin spread across Ojii-san's face and his eyes filled with delight as he joyfully declared, "It's Pochi!" Countless tiny buds adorned the branches, exuding a delightful fragrance. The Party Mice paused their lively dance, their attention captured by the blossoming buds.

In a burst of magic, the buds opened, revealing cherry blossoms at a piano glissando pace. Pink petals filled the air infusing Ojii-san's garden with joy. With a gust of wind, a cherry blossom blizzard enveloped the scene. Petals swirled and danced in a whirlwind. "What a splendid way to celebrate Pochi's life!" Ojii-san exclaimed. The Party Mice joined in, and together they journeyed through the town, following the swirling petals.

Ojii-san's cherry tree blossomed every spring thereafter, always creating a magical cherry blossom blizzard. Neighbors planted more cherry trees alongside Ojii-san's tree. Without fail, every early April, the community's cherry trees bloomed in resplendent fashion. The townspeople affectionately called Ojii-san "*Hanasaka Jii-san*," meaning "Flower Blooming Old Man." During winter, Ojii-san diligently collected fallen cherry branches, burned them, and used their ashes as fertilizer for the community's plants and flowers. He was truly an environmentalist at heart. The annual cherry blossom celebration became a cherished tradition in the town, passed down from generation to generation.

One more delightful surprise awaited Ojii-san. Among the town's numerous cherry trees, a tiny sapling sprouted right beside Ojii-san's tree. It grew leaves resembling the shape of Pochi's playful ears and a trunk that mirrored his wagging tail—it was a miniature version of Pochi! Ojii-san couldn't believe his eyes as he witnessed this adorable creation. The little Pochi tree grew alongside its parent, and every spring, it burst into its own miniature cherry blossom display, showering the area with its own unique charm.

From that day forward, Ojii-san's garden became a sanctuary. It became about more than just cherry blossoms; the garden also held memories of Pochi. The delightful sight of the Pochi tree filled Ojii-san's heart with warmth, reminding him of the love and joy they had shared. For generations to come, the town continued to celebrate the blooming cherry trees and the extraordinary story of Ojii-san and Pochi. Whenever Ojii-san sat beneath the Pochi tree, its branches swayed gently as if whispering, "Thank you, Ojii-san, for giving us a place to grow and reminding us of the beauty of friendship."

In that little corner of the world, Ojii-san lived on alongside the Pochi tree, occasionally joined by the mischievous Party Mice, forever entwined with the magical allure of the cherry blossoms tale.

Meanwhile, Obaa-san happily remained immersed in the never-ending festivities within the mysterious mice's den.

Medetashi, medetashi. Happily Ever After.

3

Ripen Persimmons

Do Your Best and Await Your Destiny ~Japanese Proverb

Saru Kani Kassen **Monkey vs. Crabs**

Original Characters: *Saru* Money, *Kani* Crab, *Kogani* Kid Crab, *Hachi* Bee, *Ishiusu* Millstone, *Kuri* Chestnut

Once upon a time, in a land filled with joy and merriment, there strolled the Kanie family with beaming smiles plastered across their faces. They were returning from the magically festive community party, a town tradition that welcomed everyone with open arms, no matter their origin. If luck happened to grace your presence in the town on that special day, you were automatically welcome to take part in the extravaganza. There were no flashy advertisements, but word of the town party had spread like wildfire because of the irresistibly scrumptious food, the lively and fun-loving crowd, the breathtaking cherry trees, and, wait for it... live mice entertainment! Yes, you heard that right! The party had everything, even mice that knew how to put on a show!

The party's host was the infamous Cherry Blooming Old Man, *Hanasaka*. On the surface, the Cherry Blooming Old Man was just a regular, somewhat lonely fellow who threw occasional parties. Only a limited number of people knew a hint of his unbelievable magical experiences. But none of those experiences were important today; this community gathering was his way of celebrating the ties that bound them all together.

For one particular family, specifically Ms. Kanie and her mischievous son, Kogani, this event had become an invaluable treat in their lives. They were the party regulars, the ones who never missed a beat. To them, the entire community had become an extension of their own family. They never doubted for a moment that anyone remotely harmful could exist in the enchanting place they called home.

As the festivities drew to a close on that particular day, Kogani received a special souvenir from *Hanasaka* —a mouthwatering *onigiri* rice ball. Now, let's be real here. It might have only been a humble rice ball, but at that moment, Kogani saw it as the equivalent of receiving a golden ticket to Willy Wonka's chocolate factory. It was a simple token, but one that held the power to transport Kogani back to the magical moments he had experienced throughout the day. With their hearts full of joy and their tummies full of delicious treats, the happy Kanie family made their way home, cherishing the memories they had created at the extraordinary party.

Out of nowhere, Ms. Saruta appeared with a mischievous grin on her face, catching Ms. Kanie completely off guard. Her sudden appearance, accompanied by a playful wave, prompted a friendly chuckle from Ms. Kanie at the unexpected surprise. Ms. Saruta exclaimed, "Well, hello there, Kanie family! How are you both doing? Oh my, that rice ball looks absolutely divine!" Kogani beamed with pride and replied, "Yep, it's my special treat for tomorrow's lunch!"

Curiosity sparked in Ms. Saruta's eyes as she leaned in closer to Kogani. She wore a quizzical expression as she asked, "Kogani, have you ever heard of the word 'investment'? You see, I have something quite extraordinary here." With a dramatic flair, she revealed a tiny persimmon seed held delicately in her palm. She continued, "If you invest in this little seed, you'll have an entire tree blooming with hundreds of juicy persimmons! No more settling for just one rice ball. I rarely sell these, but your mom has raised you to be incredibly smart, so I'm willing to make this bright persimmon seed exchange with you."

Kogani's mind raced with staggering possibilities as he thought about the offer. He glanced at his mother, who nodded encouragingly, silently conveying, "The choice is yours, my dear." Ms. Kanie understood that Ms. Saruta had not been present at the party, and she empathized with her neighbor's hunger and loneliness. Besides, what harm could trading one little rice ball do to her son's feelings? Although Kogani was only five years old, he surprised them both with his maturity when he calmly accepted Ms. Saruta's proposal.

Beaming with excitement, Ms. Saruta exclaimed, "What a brilliantly smart decision, Kogani! You're destined to become a persimmon tycoon in no time! Make sure to plant it right away and water it every single day!" She then took a hefty bite of the rice ball, relishing its deliciousness. "Mmm, absolutely scrumptious!" With a satisfied grin, Ms. Saruta turned on her heels and left Ms. Kanie and Kogani behind. Little did they know, she muttered under her breath, "Well, that was far too easy of a trick to play! Don't they know how long it takes for persimmon fruits to grow? Lucky me coming across such blissfully ignorant folks."

"Mother, can you feel how excited I am? I know our tree is going to have lots of persimmons soon! They'll be ripe and tasty. It's amazing how our tree will grow such yummy treats for us. I can't wait to pick them and have a delicious snack!" Kogani's eyes shimmered with anticipation, his imagination running wild with visions of succulent fruits.

Ms. Kanie, not wanting to dampen her little adventurer's spirit, decided to play along. She smiled warmly and replied, "Oh, indeed, it's absolutely thrilling! Let's start by germinating the seed in a small tray." They carefully nestled the precious seed within a cotton cocoon, eagerly awaiting signs of life. And lo-and-behold, in just a couple of days, the seed sprouted, bursting forth with vitality. Kogani couldn't contain his joy as he gently transplanted the seedling into the garden in front of their house, lovingly surrounding it with a miniature greenhouse.

Now, my dear readers, in the ordinary world, it usually takes around four to seven years for a persimmon tree to bear fruit. But hold onto your hats, because this is no ordinary tale! In this whimsical folktale, the magical persimmon seed little Kogani received from an obnoxious liar grew at an astonishing speed. It defied all expectations! Within a mere week, Kogani had to remove the small greenhouse because the tree's growth was unstoppable! And to their astonishment, the Kanie family discovered clusters of tiny, green persimmon fruits adorning the branches. Not just one or two, but several!

"Mother, we truly are becoming persimmon tycoons, just like Ms. Saruta said! Isn't she simply wonderful?" Kogani exclaimed. His innocent enthusiasm was infectious. He couldn't contain his excitement and rushed to share the incredible news with their neighbors, Ms. Hatch, Mr. Usui, and Ms. Kurihara. Now, these folks were well aware of Ms. Saruta's reputation for being less than trustworthy. However, in light of Kogani's news, they set aside their reservations and wholeheartedly celebrated the success of a little boy. Laughter echoed through the neighborhood as they marveled at the miraculous growth of the persimmon tree.

Two weeks had passed, and the persimmon fruits had ripened to perfection. The Kanie family eagerly gathered a ladder and a basket, preparing themselves to harvest the bountiful fruits. However, much to their dismay, the persimmon tree had grown so tall that even with the ladder, reaching the fruits was an impossible task. Disappointment clouded Kogani's face as he muttered, "Darn it, what are we going to do?"

Just then, Ms. Saruta strolled by. Her eyes widened in amazement as she exclaimed, "Well, well, look at this beauty! It's only been a couple of weeks, and yet, the tree has flourished!" Unable to believe what she was seeing, Ms. Saruta was genuinely impressed. Kogani sighed and lamented, "Indeed, Ms. Saruta, but no one can reach the persimmons since they're way up high." His voice was heavy with disappointment.

But Ms. Saruta, ever the confident one, looked at Kogani and declared, "Not a problem at all, my dear boy! Back in the old days, I used to be a champion tree climber. I'd be more than happy to help you harvest those delectable fruits!" Without hesitation, she ascended the ladder as far as it would reach, then smoothly climbed up the tree trunk, gracefully perching herself on the first sturdy branch. With skilled hands, she plucked the plumpest orange fruit, took a big, satisfying bite, and revealed her gleaming teeth, delighted by its sweetness.

From the ground below, Kogani and Ms. Kanie clapped their hands in joy, their curiosity piqued. "Is it as good as it looks?" Kogani asked eagerly. Ms. Saruta, her mouth still full of the delicious fruit, nodded vigorously and replied, "Oh, yes! It's juicy, sweet, and exceptionally splendid! I've never tasted such sweet persimmons in my entire life!" The Kanie family exchanged glances, their hearts filled with a sense of accomplishment. They were on their way to becoming true persimmon connoisseurs.

With excitement brimming within him, Kogani turned to Ms. Saruta and said, "Ms. Saruta, we have a basket ready to collect the persimmons. Would you kindly drop them down?" But much to their surprise, Ms. Saruta rudely ignored the little boy and continued to indulge in the ripe fruits. Kogani's patience wore thin, and he raised his voice, shouting, "Ms. Saruta, can you hear me? We're ready to catch the persimmons! Please start dropping them!"

Irritated by Kogani's persistence, Ms. Saruta's temper flared. She snapped back, "You're just too greedy! You don't deserve these fruits!"

With those words, she grabbed some unripe, hard persimmons and hurled them forcefully at Ms. Kanie and Kogani. "Ms. Saruta, what on earth are you doing? Stop throwing those hard fruits! It's dangerous!" Ms. Kanie exclaimed, her concern evident.

Unfortunately, their pleas fell on deaf ears. Realizing the danger, the Kanie family decided it was time to step back from the scene. But it was too late. Crash! "Ouch!" One of the green persimmons struck Ms. Kanie's head, causing her to stumble and collapse to the ground. Panic engulfed Kogani as he screamed, "Mother!"

The commotion caught the attention of their neighbor, Ms. Hatch, who quickly emerged from her house. "Kogani, what happened?" she asked urgently. Fighting back tears, Kogani stammered, "My mother... she got hit by the persimmon." Ms. Hatch, still dressed in her police officer uniform from work, sprang into action. "Stay calm, Kogani. I'll call for an ambulance right away." She swiftly reached for her walkie-talkie and dispatched the local ambulance, making sure help was on its way. Meanwhile, Mr. Usui, another concerned neighbor who had heard the raised voices, emerged from his house. "Ms. Hatch, what's going on?" he inquired, sensing the tension in the air.

"Mr. Usui, please grab an ice pack while we wait for the ambulance," Ms. Hatch instructed, balancing her phone on her shoulder. "Of course," Mr. Usui replied, hurrying off to find the ice pack. As fate would have it, Ms. Kurihara, who had just returned from her grocery shopping, stumbled upon the chaotic scene. "Kogani, are you alright?" she urgently asked. With tears streaming down his face, Kogani sadly responded, "My mother was hit by the persimmon that Ms. Saruta threw." Ms. Kurihara looked up at the persimmon tree, but all she saw were hundreds of persimmon fruits hanging from the branches.

Meanwhile, Ms. Saruta swung from the branch to a nearby rooftop, and continued to travel by rooftop until skillfully landing on her own house. "My goodness, that was a close call," she muttered to herself. After wiping the persimmon juice off her shirt with a wet towel, she settled down for a nap, completely satisfied with her actions.

Later that day, Ms. Kanie stirred in the hospital bed, her eyes fluttering open weakly. She gazed at Kogani and asked, "Where am I?" Kogani, his voice trembling with a mix of concern and excitement, explained, "Mother, you're in the hospital because the persimmon that Ms. Saruta threw knocked you down." Ms. Kanie mumbled the word "persimmon" as her memory struggled to piece together the events. Standing behind Kogani, Ms. Kurihara reassured Ms. Kanie, "You must rest, Ms. Kanie. We'll take care of your son and everything else. Don't worry." Before Ms. Kurihara could finish, Ms. Kanie drifted back into a deep sleep.

Ms. Kurihara, the determined and sharp-witted neighbor, refused to let the matter rest. She knew that justice needed to be served by the Kanie family. Knocking on Ms. Saruta's door, she called out, "Hello, Ms. Saruta. Are you home?" Ms. Saruta appeared, her expression guarded as she asked, "Yeah, I'm here. What brings you to my doorstep, Ms. Kurihara? How can I assist you?"

Ms. Kurihara wasted no time and got straight to the point. Her voice firm, she stated, "I heard you threw a hard persimmon at Ms. Kanie. Is this true? She is currently receiving hospital treatment for a concussion." Ms. Saruta's expression shifted, a mask of concern replacing her defensive demeanor. She responded, "Oh my goodness, is that true? I'm so sorry to hear about Ms. Kanie's condition. But I assure you, I would never commit such a horrible act. Why would I?"

Refusing to be swayed, Ms. Kurihara replied, "Kogani told us what happened." Ms. Saruta quickly dismissed Kogani's account, blurting, "He's only five years old. Children often have difficulty recalling events, especially in stressful situations like this. I was at home, sleeping because I was utterly exhausted. I haven't stepped foot outside today." Ms. Saruta intensely denied all the accusations Ms. Kurihara had presented. Finally, she challenged Ms. Kurihara, saying, "Ms. Kurihara, if you insist on these claims, show me hard evidence that proves I was at the scene."

Ms. Kurihara, not only a heroic neighbor but also a skilled lawyer specializing in personal injury cases, knew Ms. Saruta had a point. She needed concrete evidence to back up Kogani's story. As she gazed up at the persimmon tree, she realized that there had been no one else there to witness the incident. How could she prove Kogani's claims?

Determined to uncover the truth, Kurihara sought Ms. Hatch, the local police officer who had been present at the scene. "Ms. Hatch, we must investigate this case thoroughly. If Kogani's account is accurate, then Ms. Saruta has been bullying and assaulting the Kanie family. We need to restore justice for them," Ms. Kurihara declared, her voice filled with resolve. Ms. Hatch, understanding the gravity of the situation, responded, "I agree, Ms. Kurihara. The case is already open, and we will conduct a swift and thorough investigation to bring the truth to light."

As they delved deeper into the details, a breakthrough emerged. They discovered that there was a security camera in Ms. Kanie's home. The footage was crystal clear—Ms. Saruta climbed the ladder and skillfully hopped onto the tree. "Ms. Saruta claimed she was asleep all day, but it's clearly a lie," Ms. Hatch informed Ms. Kurihara. However, the security camera had not captured the most vicious act of throwing the persimmons, as it occurred higher than the camera's range. "It's a magnificent piece of evidence, but we need something more substantial. We must dig deeper," Ms. Hatch reported. She assured Ms. Kurihara that she was determined to uncover the truth and bring justice to the Kanie family.

The police quickly assembled a top-notch crime scene investigation team. The team rode high in a bucket truck to investigate the persimmon tree. Before beginning their ascent to the tree, Kogani pleaded with the team to pick some persimmons he and his mother had grown. Initially hesitant, the team's sympathy for the family won them over, and they agreed to help. They harvested as many plump, shiny orange persimmons as they could, providing a slight consolation to the Kanie family.

The team's investigation found clear evidence pointing towards Ms. Saruta's involvement. They discovered fingerprints along the trail leading to the top of the tree, identified cotton fibers from Ms. Saruta's shirt, collected hair samples, and found persimmon fruit juice on the branches. With these crucial pieces of evidence in hand, Ms. Hatch declared, "Now, we need to match them to Ms. Saruta's DNA." Ms.

Kurihara, determined to gather the evidence, asserted, "I will get a search warrant from the judge."

The subsequent legal proceedings progressed smoothly and quickly compared to typical criminal cases, from the arrest, to the arraignment, to the jury selections, and all the way up to the day of the trial. Ms. Saruta's defense lawyer did his best, but he couldn't match the talent and skill of Ms. Kurihara as an attorney. Despite the overwhelming evidence, including Ms. Saruta's own DNA match, Ms. Saruta's defense team insisted on pleading not guilty to all charges, disregarding the substantial evidence presented against her. This stubborn stance left a negative impression on the jury, further damaging Ms. Saruta's case. However, Ms. Saruta remained committed to living with her lie throughout the entire judicial process.

During the hearing, the jury read the charges against Ms. Saruta, who was faced with first-degree reckless endangerment of the Kanie family. This meant that Ms. Saruta was not only found guilty but also held responsible for all the Kanie family's medical expenses, lost wages, pain and suffering, and property damage. The financial burden amounted to thirty million yen (roughly three hundred thousand dollars) in cash. Losing her status as a homeowner would be a consequence of Ms. Saruta's actions, but she would still be provided with shelter and food during her time in jail. Mr. Usui, the judge from their own town, announced, "The case is closed!" With one sharp bang of the gavel, the sound reverberated through the courtroom. In the end, the Kanie family's pursuit of justice had been successful, bringing closure to a painful chapter in their lives.

The news of the verdict quickly spread throughout the community, generating a sense of relief and satisfaction. The Kanie family was once again embraced by their community, their faith in justice restored. Amidst the jubilant atmosphere, one figure stood out above all—the legendary Cherry Blooming Old Man and his troupe of Party Mice. These tiny creatures, donned in colorful costumes, were known for their infectious enthusiasm. Together, they paraded through the streets, captivating the attention of everyone they passed.

Cheers and laughter welcomed them as they arrived at the Kanie family's home, led by their vibrant procession. Under the shade of the majestic persimmon tree, Mr. Usui, Ms. Hatch, and Ms. Kurihara joined in the celebration. They twirled and spun, trying their best to match the agility of the Party Mice who flitted around them, their tiny feet tapping to an invisible beat. The sight was both enchanting and comical, especially as Ms. Kanie's movements became a hilarious imitation of the nimble creatures. The occasion was filled with pure joy that the Kanie family long deserved.

Medetashi, medetashi. Happily Ever After.

4

Dango Sweet Rice Cakes

One Opportunity, One Encounter ~Japanese Proverb

M*omotaro* Peach Boy

Once upon a time, in the mystical land of Western Japan, there lived a childless Ojii-san (Old man) and Obaa-san (Old Woman). Tired of the hustle and bustle of urban Tokyo, they decided to embark on a new adventure as white peach farmers in their "Second Life." They purchased a picturesque property on a slope, which made it quite a challenge for two elderly folks to hike up and down. But hey, who needs a stair climber when you're as fit as these two were?

Soon, those dainty pink flowers transformed into tiny fruits, adorning the branches of the peach trees. Noticing this, Obaa-san overflowed with elation and shouted, "Ojii-san, look! We have peaches! Our hard work has paid off!" Ojii-san smiled proudly and replied, "Indeed! Now it's time to prepare the paper bags."

After finishing their field work, Ojii-san and Obaa-san turned their attention to crafting paper bags from old newspapers. They carefully cut rectangles, folded them in half, and glued the sides, creating perfect envelopes to protect the peaches from mischievous insects and hungry birds. Every day, they lovingly covered each peach, ensuring its safe and undisturbed growth. And every night, they diligently made new paper envelopes for the tender fruits.

After two weeks of their meticulous mission, the task was finally complete. Like proud parents, they admired their handiwork, hoping for each fruit to grow healthy, sweet, and juicy. As they bid goodnight to their covered peaches, Ojii-san and Obaa-san returned home with hearts full of pride.

On their way back home, the tired but content couple stumbled upon an unusual sight. Three garden snakes slithered across the path, seemingly fleeing from something. Ojii-san scratched his head in confusion, muttering, "My goodness, not one, but three snakes? That's odd." And if that wasn't peculiar enough, they encountered not just one, but multiple families of deer—three adult deer and five adorable fawns—frolicking among the peach trees. Obaa-san chuckled and quipped, "Looks like we stumbled upon a deer party! Who knew they were such party animals?" It was indeed a strange sight, but exhausted from their peach-bagging adventures, they decided to continue their journey home.

The couple enjoyed a simple traditional Japanese meal, indulged in a hot, soothing tub, and retired to bed. Unbeknownst to them, a vicious typhoon was lurking, ready to strike that very night. The animals, with their instinctive nature, had been trying to warn them, but Ojii-san and Obaa-san had felt too accomplished to sense their signals. Worse, the old couple was long-time disconnected from the world of television, internet, and social media because they had chosen a life of simplicity and appreciation, embracing each day as it came, even the unpredictable weather. Little did they know that the peculiar behavior of the animals was a forewarning of the impending natural disaster.

The following morning, Obaa-san ventured outside and encountered a sight that left her trembling in utter shock. With her heart racing and her voice shaking, she said, "Goodness gracious! What in the world?!" The scene before her was beyond anything she could have imagined, a stunning spectacle that defied all logic and comprehension.

The aftermath of the storm had transformed their once serene surroundings into a chaotic scene of destruction. Flower pots lay shattered, their vibrant blossoms scattered across the ground. The front yard was a mess, with debris rolling about, and the neighboring chickens had taken advantage of the disarray, making themselves at home. Ojii-san emerged from the house, his eyes filled with disbelief as he beheld the truth before him.

"Our peaches..." he uttered, his voice heavy with despair. The couple hurriedly made their way to their cherished peach hill, their hearts pounding in anticipation of the potential devastation they were about to witness. And what they saw was truly heartbreaking.

Their beloved peach trees, once adorned with almost ripe fruits, now stood stripped and forlorn. Wet newspapers, muddied by the storm, were scattered arbitrarily. Hundreds of nearly mature peaches lay strewn about, casualties of the destructive forces of nature. Some even floated aimlessly in the irrigation, a stark indication of the devastation that had occurred. Obaa-san's heart shattered as she beheld the scene, her tears flowing uncontrollably.

They both stood there in shock, witnessing the painful sight of their beloved peaches floating away in the stream. Obaa-san's tears continued to stream down her face, mirroring the sorrow in her heart. Brokenhearted, Obaa-san aimlessly reached into the irrigation stream where fallen peaches bobbed gently in the current. She could feel the cold water caressing the peaches as they drifted away, bidding a sorrowful farewell.

Among the floating peaches, one stubborn fruit refused to leave Obaa-san's grasp. It clung to her thumb as if pleading to be rescued. She gazed at it in awe and noticed a mesmerizing golden glow emanating from within. Obaa-san, captivated by the mysterious peach in her hand, turned toward him and exclaimed, "Look, Ojii-san! This peach is glowing!"

Curiosity mixed with skepticism adorned Ojii-san's face as he drew closer to examine the peculiar fruit. He wondered why it emitted a radiant golden light and expressed his doubts about its authenticity.

Realizing that they might be deluding themselves in their grief-stricken state, Obaa-san suggested they take deep breaths to regain their composure. The couple closed their eyes, inhaled and exhaled slowly, and tried to find peace amidst the chaos and confusion. With each successive breath, the golden peach on Obaa-san's thumb seemed to react, wiggling and pulsating with a brighter light. Then, Ojii-san and Obaa-san opened their eyes and exchanged bewildered glances, unsure of what they were witnessing. As they took another deep breath, the golden peach split open, revealing an astonishing sight—a tiny, wailing baby nestled within its glowing core. "It's a boy!" Obaa-san exclaimed.

Ojii-san's eyes widened in disbelief. But it was true. Both realized that this miraculous baby had just been born from the very heart of the golden peach. Overwhelmed with joy, Obaa-san wrapped him in a towel and gently cradled the baby in her arms. Overjoyed with delight, Obaa-san declared, "What an adorable baby! Ojii-san, this is our baby!"

The couple stood there, marveling at the miracle that had unfolded before them. In that moment, they forgot about the devastation of their peach harvest and embraced the newfound joy of parenthood.

"There he is, our little miracle, born from the heart of a peach! Let's name him *Momo* (Peach) *Taro* (Boy)!" Ojii-san proposed, his eyes twinkling with mischief. Obaa-san's face lit up like a thousand fireworks on a summer night. "Oh, what a stroke of genius!" she exclaimed, her delight contagious. "Momotaro, my sweet peach boy, you've come into our lives like a ray of sunshine amidst a storm. May you grow to possess a heart as vast as the ocean, a mind as sharp as a samurai's sword, and a body as sturdy as Mount *Fuji*. We will love you until the end of time!"

And so it happened, in a miraculous twist of fate. With a stretch and a yawn that defied the laws of nature, Momotaro transformed from a tiny infant to a strapping young lad, as if the universe had pressed the fast-forward button for Ojii-san and Obaa-san's viewing pleasure. They stood in awe, witnessing the magical spectacle unfolding before their eyes.

"Magnificent!" Ojii-san exclaimed, his voice filled with awe. Momotaro, with a heart brimming with love, gathered his beloved parents in his bulging arms. The trio shared a moment of pure joy, as if they had stumbled into the plot of a heartwarming Japanese *anime*.

Obaa-san, her face beaming with pride, busied herself in the kitchen, preparing a feast fit for the heavens. *Onigiri* rice balls and *kibi dango*, lovingly crafted by her nimble hands, adorned the table. Each bite that Momotaro savored seemed to fortify his muscles and sharpen his intellect, as if every morsel carried the secrets of strength and wisdom.

But alas, the day brought a harsh reminder of the cruel reality they faced. Ojii-san let out a heavy sigh, his heart burdened with the weight of their misfortune. Obaa-san, ever the optimist, interjected with a glimmer of hope, "Ojii-san, let us first clean up this mess. Once we've swept away the debris, a path forward will reveal itself. Our peach trees may be battered, but their spirits remain unbroken!"

With a determined nod, Momotaro joined the conversation, his resolve shining through. "Don't worry, I will help you! Together, we shall overcome any obstacle!" With rakes in hand and compost bags slung over their shoulders, the determined trio ascended the peach hill. Momotaro, fueled by an unseen energy, set a blistering pace, effortlessly out-raking Ojii-san and Obaa-san by a factor of ten.

In a remarkable display of teamwork, the muddy newspapers and fallen peaches were swiftly cleared, transforming the chaotic mess into a pristine landscape in just a few hours. "Thank you, Momotaro. Your strength knows no bounds!" Obaa-san exclaimed, beaming with pride. "And not just that, your raking skills are seriously impressive! I'm in awe!" Ojii-san exclaimed, marveling at Momotaro's incredible abilities. In the midst of the cleanup, Momotaro stumbled upon a torn piece of newspaper from the peach bag, which caught his attention.

"Ojii-san, Obaa-san, take a look at this! It's a newspaper scrap talking about *Onigashima* Island, the infamous Ogre Island," Momotaro revealed, a curious glint in his eye. "What's the scoop, my dear?" Obaa-san inquired, her curiosity sparked. Momotaro's brows furrowed as he delved into his findings. "From what I can gather, the islanders are living in fear of these *oni*, these ogres. I wonder what they've been up to."

"*Oni,* Ogres? If they truly exist, we must ensure the safety of the islanders. Momotaro, my boy, why don't you go and investigate?" Ojii-san suggested, concern etched on his face. "But I promised to help you clean the peach hill," Momotaro replied dutifully, his sense of responsibility tugging at his heartstrings. Obaa-san pulled him into a warm embrace and said, "Momotaro, my courageous child, I am bursting with pride for the person you are. Ojii-san is right, someone must shed light on the mysteries of *Onigashima* Island. Cleaning the peach hill will take a considerable amount of time, even with your immense strength. By utilizing both your muscles and your sharp mind, you can aid the islanders in their time of need! Let me prepare a special treat, *Kibidango*, infused with our love and strength, to accompany you on your journey."

The following morning, as the first rays of dawn painted the sky with hues of pink and gold, Obaa-san sprang into action. With nimble fingers, she crafted numerous *Kibidango*, pouring her love into each delicate creation. Addressing Momotaro, she spoke with tender affection.

"Momotaro, my dear, these Kibidango are no ordinary delicacies. Remember to share them generously, spreading your love and compassion wherever you go." Momotaro nodded, packing the precious *Kibidango* along with his supplies—ample water, a trusty map, a towel, a journal, a pencil, and a knife—into his trusty backpack.

"*Itte-kimasu*! I am ready to go!" Momotaro announced, his voice brimming with determination. Ojii-san and Obaa-san, their hearts heavy with a mix of worry and pride, bid him farewell. "*Itte-rasshai*! Good luck! Take care," they called out in unison.

Setting his sights on the northeastern horizon, Momotaro embarked on his strenuous journey. Day after day, he trudged along the winding paths, from one town to another, never faltering in his determination. But halfway to *Onigashima* Island, Momotaro found himself approaching a small homeless camp. Modest cardboard box shelters dotted the area, and there, in front of a particularly elaborate cardboard structure, sat a man who appeared to be down on his luck. Momotaro, ever compassionate, couldn't ignore the man's plea for rations.

"Excuse me, sir. Do you have something to eat?" the man inquired, his eyes filled with a mix of hunger and desperation. Momotaro's heart swelled with empathy as he gazed at the man. "I may not have much, but I can share one of my precious *Kibi-dango* with you. My name is Momotaro. And what is your name?" The man's weary eyes brightened at the prospect of nourishment and human connection. As he met Momotaro's gaze, he mustered the courage to speak.

"My name is Inukai," he revealed, his voice tinged with a hint of sadness. "Once, I was an esteemed architect with my own thriving office. But a treacherous business partner left me drowning in a sea of debt. To ensure the survival of my wife and daughter, I sent them away to a place where they could find financial stability. The relentless debt collectors seized everything: my car, my office, and my home. Now all I have left to construct are these flimsy cardboard walls." Moved by Inukai's plight, Momotaro sat beside him, their souls intertwining through shared stories of hardship and loss. Inukai's words resonated deeply within Momotaro's heart, prompting him to share the purpose of his journey—to *Onigashima* Island, a place shrouded in mystery and danger.

Gratitude radiated from Inukai's eyes as he expressed his appreciation. "Thank you, Momotaro, for your kindness in sharing the *Kibi-dango*. Your act of generosity has rekindled a spark within me, igniting a desire to take action instead of merely existing within these cardboard walls. I shall accompany you on your journey, offering whatever help I can provide."

As Inukai and Momotaro prepared to rise from their spot, a figure emerged from another cardboard house, strolling casually towards them. To their astonishment, the person had her eyes fixed on Momotaro's backpack as she attempted to snatch it away. Inukai's protective instincts flared, and he bellowed at the intruder, swiftly seizing her arm and reclaiming the stolen backpack.

"Settle down, Inukai-san," Momotaro reassured, his voice calm yet firm. He then turned to the intruder and addressed her directly. "Hey there, I'm Momotaro. And what is your name?" She looked down, her voice trembling with shame. "Saruta," she muttered, her words barely audible. Undeterred by her attempted theft, Momotaro extended an olive branch of kindness. "Saruta-san, there's no need to resort to stealing. If you're hungry, I'd be more than happy to share one of my *Kibi-dango* with you."

Tears welled up in Saruta's eyes as she gratefully accepted the offered *Kibi-dango*. It had been weeks since she had last eaten, explaining the desperation that led her to such drastic measures. Overwhelmed with emotion, Saruta made a solemn pledge.

"Thank you, Momotaro-san. This *Kibi-dango* is not only delicious but feels like a source of strength. I feel stronger than ever before. Please allow me to accompany you on your journey and lend my assistance," Saruta bowed deeply, her gratitude evident. But Saruta had another person in mind who could benefit from the power-packed kibidango—someone named Kiji, living in the last cardboard house. Eager to extend the same kindness that was bestowed upon her, Saruta beckoned her newfound companions to follow.

Momotaro, Inukai, and Saruta approached Kiji's cardboard home, calling out to him. A voice responded from within, and as they turned, they beheld Kiji emerging from the shadows. A fist bump between Saruta and Kiji signified their connection, their camaraderie apparent.

"Hey, Kiji! I heard you might be hungry, and I'd be delighted to share my *Kibi-dango* with you," Momotaro approached with a warm smile. Grateful for any sustenance, Kiji expressed his thanks. "Whatever is edible will do wonders. Thank you. And what is your name?" "My name is Momotaro," he replied, a sense of mystery enveloping his words. "They say I was born from a magical golden peach after a massive typhoon. So, I might possess some sort of magical power, although I haven't quite figured it out yet. What I do know is that I am on a mission to ensure the well-being of the villagers and confront the oni, the ogres, on Onigashima Island. I hope the *Kibi-dango* fills your empty stomach and infuses you with energy and positivity." Impressed by Momotaro's resolve, Kiji made a heartfelt request. "Please allow me to join you on your journey and lend my assistance. Together, we can face whatever lies ahead."

The group expanded, forged by shared experiences, fortitude, and the power of nourishment. Momotaro, Inukai, Saruta, and Kiji set forth, a united force ready to tackle the challenges of Onigashima Island, their individual strengths magnified by their unwavering bond.

"Wow, I've been walking all alone for so long, and now I've found three amazing friends! How fortunate I am!" Momotaro excitedly scribbled in his journal. Unbeknownst to him, his backpack had a magical quality. No matter how many *Kibi-dango* he consumed or shared, it never seemed to diminish. He marveled at the replenishing supply, though he never suspected any enchantment. The group continued their journey, walking day after day, until finally, after many weeks, they arrived at the port to *Onigashima* Island.

"Momotaro-san, I see a fisherman's row boat over there. I suggest we approach them and inquire if they would be willing to let us use it," Saruta suggested. Employing her diplomatic skills, she engaged in negotiations with the fishermen and managed to secure their cooperation. With their newly acquired mode of transportation, Momotaro, Inukai, Saruta, and Kiji boarded the boat and embarked on their journey towards Onigashima Island, braving the tumultuous and untamed ocean. As the saying goes, "Nothing is impossible," and true to those words, Team Momotaro successfully navigated the challenging voyage to reach Onigashima Island. "We've made it! Onigashima, here we come!"

Onigashima Island, on sunny days, showcased its true beauty as a captivating island. On the day Team Momotaro arrived, the sun was shining brightly, filling them with joy and excitement. They exchanged celebratory high fives, reveling in the favorable weather. Kiji, eager as ever, was the first to disembark from the boat and pull it ashore onto the sandy beach. The rest of the team followed suit, lending their strength to push the boat in place. As they made their way forward, they encountered a breathtaking sight—a mesmerizing display of three-dimensional *zen* beach art crafted from rocks and sea glass. The art was intricately embedded in the sand, solid and unyielding. They marveled at how this masterpiece flawlessly captured the grounded essence of natural materials. "Was it perhaps the work of magic? I wonder what kind of person can create something like this," Inukai pondered.

As Team Momotaro strolled through the downtown area, they attentively tuned in to the conversations of the island's inhabitants. "Did you happen to catch a glimpse of the Red Oni Ogre yesterday? Someone mentioned seeing it," a woman in a group said, attempting to grab their attention. Another person responded, "No, I haven't come across any red or green ogres, but I must admit, the mere thought of encountering an oni makes me uneasy." A third individual interjected suspiciously, "But is there any truth to these claims about ogres on our island?"

Interrupting the conversation, Momotaro stepped forward, his voice filled with concern. "Excuse me, but I couldn't help overhearing your discussion about '*Oni*.' I apologize for the interruption. My name is Momotaro, and I'm here because I came across a newspaper article mentioning Oni on this very island. I wanted to make sure everything is alright. Are you all doing okay?" "As I mentioned earlier, my friend claims to have seen one, and I'm concerned that there might be some here!" one woman shared. "What did Oni do to your friend? Why are you so enraged?" Inukai inquired. The woman stammered, "W-well, I haven't actually seen one. I suppose it's just the fear of the unknown. If they appear menacing, they might pose a threat to us."

"So, if I understand correctly, you're suggesting that, one, *Oni*'s frightening appearance implies potential harm; two, apart from your friend, no one else has witnessed *Oni*; and, three, no harm has been inflicted thus far. Am I capturing your concerns accurately?" diplomatic Saruta summarized politely.

The woman's facial expression seemed to relax a bit. Saruta continued, "Do you know where your friend spotted the Oni?" The woman replied, "Behind the temple." The second woman whispered, her right hand covering her mouth, "Nobody wants to visit that temple. It has been deserted since the passing of the last monk several years ago." The members of Team Momotaro exchanged glances. "Deserted temple," Inukai and Kiji repeated, as if savoring the bitterness in their mouths.

The temple was not far from downtown, yet it clearly appeared abandoned. "No wonder nobody wants to come here," Kiji blurted out. However, since Inukai, Saruta, and Kiji had once been homeless, they were not afraid of neglect or filth. Unlike makeshift cardboard walls, the temple's structure was solid. Inukai marveled, "This temple was designed and constructed in the 1200s. It definitely needs some tender loving care, but just look at the beauty of its architecture—the black tiled roof and the lion statues." Momotaro was impressed and remarked, "Indeed, you possess an extensive knowledge of architecture."

Suddenly, rustling sounds emerged from the bushes near the temple building. The woman's claims may prove to hold some truth after all. "Well, it looks like we might have some Oni roommates here," Kiji remarked, his detective senses tingling with excitement. Following the noise, Kiji discovered a path hidden amidst the tall, dried grass behind the building. With a keen intuition and an agile spring in his step, Kiji listened to his gut and swiftly pursued the man-made trail. One step, two steps, three steps, four steps, and just as he was about to take the fifth step, thud! Something darted across his path. Kiji was about to give chase when he realized it was a terrified deer, bounding away into the depths of the woods. "Phew," Inukai sighed with relief.

Momotaro gathered his team and suggested, "I don't think we should startle the Oni, if they truly exist. They haven't done anything harmful, and people are frightened simply because of their appearance. When we encounter them, let's keep our cool." "All right, Momotaro-san," they all agreed, ready to follow his lead. Saruta chimed in with a suggestion,

"Why don't we clean up this property and wait for them to return? It might help them understand that our intentions are not to harm them."

"That's a great idea," Momotaro acknowledged, pleased with Saruta's proposal.

It was rather comical to think that the *Oni* were scared of a group of humans, rather than the other way around as the newspapers had reported. Nevertheless, it was evident that the Oni were too afraid to make an appearance. The team got to work, first tackling the daunting task of removing all the overgrown weeds surrounding the temple building. It proved to be quite a challenge since no one had tended to the area for several consecutive years. After three long hours of determined effort, they successfully cleared away the weeds and restored the temple's majestic presence, which now sat proudly, free from the shackles of unruly grass.

Meanwhile, Kiji ventured back into downtown to borrow cleaning tools from the Coffee/Ice Cream shop. Armed with the necessary supplies, the team diligently set to work inside the temple hall, dusting, wiping, and scrubbing away every trace of dirt. Not a hint of filth remained. In addition to their cleaning efforts, Team Momotaro decided to dig a deep hole and construct a brand new outhouse for convenience. As the sun began its descent towards the horizon, all the cleaning tasks were successfully completed.

Surveying the transformed temple property, they noticed the presence of numerous abandoned family tombstones alongside the temple building itself. Team Momotaro put their hands together to show respect to the long forgotten ancestors. Then, they took it upon themselves to clear the overgrown grasses and create an open area for a cozy campfire. "Let's camp out here tonight. It's nice and clean," Momotaro suggested to his team, sensing the pleasant atmosphere that now surrounded them. As darkness blanketed the land, exhaustion caught up with them all, and one by one, they succumbed to a deep and restful slumber beneath the tranquil night sky.

In the early morning light, Saruta stirred from her slumber and caught sight of a pair of shadows near the temple building. With her curiosity piqued, she approached cautiously, her steps deliberate and silent. Inside the temple hall, she discovered a red-bodied figure and a green-bodied figure, seated cross-legged side by side. Were they meditating, or were they mere statues? Saruta climbed the three steps, carefully making her way onto the temple floor. She settled herself behind the two figures, closed her eyes, and began to focus on her breath.

To her surprise, a voice, gentle and tranquil, echoed within Saruta's mind. "Thank you for taking care of the temple," it whispered. Saruta questioned whether she had truly heard the voice or if it was simply a figment of her imagination. But then, the soft voice continued, pouring out its confession.

"We are the last two *Oni* on *Onigashima* Island. People were oblivious to our existence as they developed and shaped this island according to their desires. The Red *Oni* wished to coexist harmoniously with humans, but their fear of our appearance drove them away. We understood that they were unaware of our presence, yet their actions amounted to an invasion of our island, effectively ridding it of the *Oni*. Humans were too frightened to engage with us, even though we harbored no ill intent. As soon as they laid eyes on us, they would hurl objects or flee in terror. It was unjust, but it became our reality.

"And so, we made the decision to retreat and live in seclusion, hidden away in a place where no one would venture. Occasionally, the Red *Oni* would venture out to observe the humans, only to be met with screams of horror. We have grown weary of being judged solely based on our appearance."

As Saruta listened to the anguished sobs, she gently opened her eyes and swallowed hard, her voice steady and comforting. "Crying *Oni*... It's alright to let your tears flow. I can only imagine how incredibly difficult it has been for you. We hear your pain, and we are here to support you. Momotaro and his team stand by your side."

The sun continued its ascent in the sky, casting a warm glow upon the scene. Saruta spoke up, her tone resolute. "Now is the time to devise a plan." As she rose to her feet, she noticed her teammates had gathered just outside the temple hall, waiting for her. "Yes, let's formulate a plan," Kiji declared with determination. The Red Oni and Green Oni exchanged smiles, sensing a glimmer of hope. The members of Team Momotaro and the two Ogres formed a circle, ready to brainstorm ideas. After several discussions and lively exchanges, an idea sparked within Momotaro's mind, prompting him to exclaim, "Yes, we can build a business!"

The next ten days flew by like a whirlwind, but in the best possible way. Momotaro took charge of opening a business account and successfully securing the necessary funds from the local bank. Inukai put his design skills to work and created a charming wooden structure resembling a cozy drive-through coffee shop-like building. Inukai and Kiji embarked on a trip to the downtown lumber store to gather supplies and tools.

Meanwhile, Momotaro took care of shopping for materials, crafting signs and price tags, and lending a hand in constructing the structure.

Saruta took on the role of instructor, guiding the Red *Oni* and Green *Oni* in essential tasks. She taught them how to trim nails, wash their hands with soap, smile without causing alarm, listen attentively without growling, and speak with a friendly tone of voice. The ogres eagerly absorbed knowledge on counting change, bookkeeping, and understanding taxes. With their newfound skills, Team Momotaro ventured downtown to offer samples of *Kibidango* to the locals. Alongside them, the Red and Green *Oni* joined the effort, doing their best to appear non-threatening. The people of Onigashima Island couldn't hide their initial fear, as they had never encountered Oni before, despite hearing tales of them throughout their lives.

Gradually, the islanders realized that the *Oni* were not as fearsome as they appeared. In fact, they were friendly and well-mannered, albeit with a hint of awkwardness. The Kibidango Sample Campaign proved to be a resounding success. Team Momotaro and the Oni eagerly awaited the official opening day of Japan's Best Kibidango, brimming with anticipation for the exciting new chapter ahead.

The much-anticipated day arrived—the grand opening of Japan's Best Kibidango. To their astonishment, a long line had formed even before the official opening time. "Oh my goodness, would you look at that line!" Red *Oni* exclaimed, wide-eyed with excitement. Green *Oni* admitted nervously, "Yeah, I'm excited too, but I can't help feeling a bit nervous." Saruta reassured them, "No worries, everyone knows how delicious Kibidango is, and they're no longer scared of *Oni.* Just remember to keep up your positive and friendly social skills!"

Momotaro chimed in, agreeing with Saruta's words. He turned to the Red *Oni* and Green *Oni* and asked with a proud smile, "Are you ready to open the store?" He handed his backpack to Green *Oni,* and together, with Red *Oni* by their side, they proclaimed in unison, "Good morning, Onigashima Island! Are you ready for Japan's Best Kibidango?"

One by one, people eagerly purchased dozens of *Kibidango* at a time. Kiji ventured out to the waiting line and placed a sign at the 100th customer, which read, "This marks the end of the morning sale. The afternoon sale will commence at 1:30 PM." This clever tactic left people with a choice—wait or risk being disappointed. Each session, they managed to sell one hundred dozen *Kibidango.* Momotaro's backpack went from full to empty, producing precisely one hundred dozen in the morning. After their lunch break, the backpack had magically refilled itself, ready to supply another hundred dozen. Red *Oni* and Green *Oni* gained confidence and found their stride through Japan's Best Kibidango. However, they couldn't help but feel a twinge of concern about what would happen when Team Momotaro eventually departed.

After a successful first week of operations, Momotaro called his team and the *Oni* together for a meeting. With joyous congratulations resonating through the air, Momotaro turned to the team and exclaimed, "Well done on the successful opening of our Kibidango business! It seems that as long as we maintain our kindness and politeness, the backpack will continue to be filled with an abundance of Kibidango. We can distribute the profits among ourselves and also allocate a portion to a worthy cause. What are your thoughts?"

Inukai eagerly shared his vision, saying, "I propose using a portion of the profits to establish a Shelter and Recovery Center for the Homeless. Having experienced homelessness firsthand, I understand the challenges they face. Together, leveraging our strengths as a team, we can make a meaningful difference." Kiji chimed in gratefully, acknowledging Saruta's impact, "Absolutely! If it weren't for Saruta introducing us to Momotaro-san, I would still be a helpless and lost soul. I'm incredibly grateful for this opportunity."

Touched by her own journey, Saruta's eyes welled up, and she spoke with heartfelt sincerity, "Once, desperation clouded my judgment, and I entertained the thought of taking Momotaro-san's backpack out of sheer hunger. I had previously lived a life of deceit and dishonesty, causing harm to numerous individuals. However, reflecting upon those times now, I am brimming with immense pride for both myself and my exceptional teammates. Together, we have formed an unbreakable bond. Thank you, Momotaro-san, and the entire team, for taking me under your wings!"

Inukai, moved by the newfound sense of purpose and camaraderie, added, "Once, I believed I had lost everything, but now I understand that true wealth lies in the love and support of a remarkable team. Thank you, Momotaro-san." Their expressions of gratitude and determination filled the room. As they embraced their shared mission, Team Momotaro knew that their journey was far from over. With their thriving Kibidango business as a foundation, they would work together to create a brighter future, not just for themselves, but for the greater good.

Red *Oni* looked at Team Momotaro with a glimmer of gratitude in his eyes and jokingly remarked, "Well, my dream has come true. Green *Oni* and I don't have to hide anymore. Just as long as I don't get too excited, I can keep these fangs in my mouth." Green *Oni* burst into laughter, enjoying the light-hearted moment.

Momotaro, with a sense of accomplishment, continued, "You are all ready to take on the world. I'll head home to visit my parents. Take care of my backpack and have a blast with your business. You are Japan's Best Team, selling Japan's Best *Kibidango*. I eagerly await the progress of the Homeless Shelter and Recovery Center."

"Momotaro-san, thank you. We already miss you," Red *Oni* expressed his gratitude. Just then, a majestic dragon with a long tail descended from the sky. Green *Oni* explained, "Momotaro-san, this dragon will take you home. She's a part of our family." The dragon gracefully scooped up Momotaro and soared above the hills, passing by the places they had climbed and the spot where the team had rowed across to the island. In a blink of an eye, it felt like a dream as the dragon gently set Momotaro down in front of Ojii-san and Obaa-san's house.

"*Tadaima*, I am home!" Momotaro joyfull announced his return."*Ok aeri*! Welcome home, Momotaro! We missed you dearly!" The three of them embraced, their happiness spilling over into tears of joy. Obaa-san chimed in, "I've just made some fresh *Kibidango*. Let's enjoy them together!"

And so, they sat down and savored Obaa-san's enchanting homemade *Kibidango*, the delightful treats that possessed a touch of magic, their flavors transporting them to a realm of pure delight.

Remarkably, Ojii-san and Obaa-san were in better shape than the average spring chicken. You see, Ojii-san had been commuting for a mind-numbing one hour and thirty minutes every day for the past forty years. His trip included twenty minutes of walking from home to the train station, and another twenty minutes from the station to the office. His daily eighty-minute stroll had become the secret to his superhuman strength.

Meanwhile, Obaa-san had her own method of keeping fit. She pedaled her way to work on her *Mama-Chari* (trusty ladies' bike), enduring a forty-minute journey each way. Her eighty minutes of daily bike riding transformed her into a powerhouse, matching Ojii-san's vitality step for step.

Armed with their extraordinary health and unwavering confidence, the old couple was ready to conquer their new peach hill. And oh, what a peachy property it was! Not only did it boast a splendid slope, but it also featured a natural irrigation creek that had been nourishing the land for centuries. This hill was practically the Garden of Eden for peaches!

The previous owners of the property were a mother and her young son, who had recently suffered the loss of their late husband and father. They had struggled to maintain the peach hill amidst their grief and decided it was time to pass on the legacy. Instead of simply accepting the highest bidder, the mother and son conducted face-to-face interviews with potential candidates, eager to find a replacement who would love and care for their plump and juicy peaches.

Enter Ojii-san and Obaa-san, with their genuine passion, farming expertise, and the vitality of superheroes in their golden years. The stars aligned, and they were chosen as the rightful owners of the beautiful Peach Hill.

Every morning, the sprightly couple would make their way up the hill, treating each peach tree as if it were their own child. As they weeded, fertilized, and prevented the infestation of pesky insects, they engaged in heartfelt conversations with their leafy offspring. Ojii-san would greet the trees with a twinkle in his eye, saying, "Good morning, beautiful trees! How did you enjoy the rain last night?" Obaa-san, full of adoration, would exclaim, "Oh, my little tree, you look absolutely stunning today! It's going to be a magnificent day for all of us!"

With their love and care, Ojii-san and Obaa-san nurtured their peach trees, turning Peach Hill into a bountiful paradise. With their whimsical conversations and unwavering dedication, they proved that you're never too old to embark on a second life filled with peaches and laughter.

Ojii-san and Obaa-san had a simple yet delightful lunch ritual: *onigiri* rice balls filled with *umeboshi*, salty sour plums, and wrapped in *nori*, black seaweed. And if they were feeling fancy, they would treat themselves to *Kibidango*, those delightful millet-powdered round rice cakes, for an afternoon snack. One day, as they savored their *onigiri* rice balls, Obaa-san couldn't contain her excitement and exclaimed, "I can't wait for the abundance of juicy peaches on each tree!" Ojii-san nodded in agreement, his mouth full of deliciousness.

When the peach trees blossomed in full splendor, the couple celebrated with a special picnic under their leafy canopy. The air was filled with the sweet aroma of the flowers, and the sight of the delicate petals brought joy to their hearts.

Medetashi, medetashi. Happily Ever After!

5

Turtles on the Beach

THE CRANE LIVES FOR A THOUSAND YEARS, WHILE THE TURTLE LIVES FOR TEN THOUSAND YEARS. ~JAPANESE PROVERB

U*rashima Taro* Seaside Boy

Once upon a time, a young boy and his mother embarked on a new adventure, leaving their past behind and finding themselves on a quaint little island nestled in the southern part of Japan. Their entire life's possessions were neatly packed into a single, miniature red moving truck. The house they arrived at was none other than a weathered cabin, once occupied by Taro's great-grandparents. The peeling exterior paint gave the humble dwelling a somewhat forlorn appearance, diminishing its true worth.

Clearly, no one had inhabited the house for many years. Tall weeds encircled the perimeter, and the trunks of the apple and Japanese pear trees were adorned with decades' worth of moss. Despite the house's dilapidation, they couldn't help but feel a sense of gratitude for its serendipitous location, blessed with the comforting scent of saltwater and the rejuvenating embrace of the sea breeze. As they strolled along the beach, the young boy and his mother were greeted by the melancholic melodies of sandpipers, their haunting songs echoing across the shore.

Taro's mother, bless her hardworking soul, toiled day in and day out. Yet, the Urashima family's piggy bank was far from overflowing with gold coins. Undeterred by their humble circumstances, they rolled up their sleeves and tackled the chores that awaited them. They mowed the property's unruly lawn, planted flowers to add a touch of color to their surroundings, and scraped away at the old paint on the house. They dreamt of the day when they could afford a fresh coat of paint to make that cabin shine like a brand new penny.

But above all, Taro and his mother cherished the most valuable treasures they possessed: each other's company and their good health. They knew that wealth wasn't just about money; it was about finding joy in the simplest of things and appreciating the blessings that came their way. And so, with determination and gratitude in their hearts, they continued their journey on the island, creating a home filled with love and laughter.

Unlike the Urashimas, who embraced a pure sense of inner peace and appreciation for their lives, their neighbor harbored a cruel streak, spreading impeccable rumors throughout the community. Tragically, these rumors found fertile ground and took root in the minds of the island's other inhabitants. "Did you know," whispered one person to another, "that Ms. Urashima is a single mom because she was cursed by her ancestors? Her husband met his untimely passing because of it."

Word traveled swiftly from one person to the next, the rumors gaining momentum with each retelling. Soon enough, the people on the island began to completely ignore Ms. Urashima. It was a stark departure from the typically polite and respectful nature of Japanese society, where even passing neighbors would be greeted with a bow or a friendly nod. But now, the entire community turned a blind eye to her. Even the cashier at the local supermarket avoided any eye contact, failing to utter a simple "thank you" as Ms. Urashima completed her purchases. Before forming any hasty judgments about the villagers, I urge you, dear readers, to consider that anyone could experience a feeling of unease if they believed their safety was at risk. Nobody wanted to take a chance at becoming a potential victim of the alleged curse. It was simply a natural instinct of self-preservation at play.

Yet, the saddest part of this tale was that no one bothered to investigate whether the "curse" rumor held any truth. No one mustered the courage to stand up and declare, "Hey, leave Urashima alone." It could have been a remarkable ending, couldn't it? This was the work of the unseen curse's cruel grip, which manipulated people's mindsets and erased all traces of their good deeds.

The insidious bullying campaign persisted even within Taro's Little League Soccer (LLS) games. In the stands, Ms. Urashima sat alone, with empty seats on either side of her. Taro, a quiet boy with limited soccer skills, had been invited to join the community's LLS team to ensure there were enough players. Despite his efforts, Taro often found himself kicking at thin air instead of the soccer ball, leading to jeers and laughter from the spectators.

On one occasion, Taro accidentally kicked another player's shin, provoking anger from the onlookers. Slowly but surely, a toxic environment of both physical and emotional bullying took hold amongst the players, all happening unbeknownst to the parents in attendance. Taro became the target of intentional trips and falls, prompting the crowd to erupt in cheers. Through it all, Ms. Urashima bit her tongue, never engaging in arguments or confrontation.

Remarkably, neither Ms. Urashima nor Taro allowed themselves to be consumed by unhappiness or anger. This only served to infuriate those around them even more. Perhaps these individuals were envious of Ms. Urashima's unwavering serenity and Taro's unyielding resilience, which they consistently displayed despite the adversity they faced.

The Urashima mother-and-son duo found immense joy in their daily ritual of beach combing. Like clockwork, every morning and evening, they ventured out to the shore, eager to immerse themselves in the wonders it held. Together, they embarked on leisurely strolls, their eyes trained on the sandy expanse before them.

As Taro, the young boy with an adventurous spirit, busied himself with digging deep holes and constructing elaborate sandcastles, his mother, Ms. Urashima, delved into her own artistic pursuits. With great care, she meticulously arranged her treasured collection of smooth rocks and shimmering sea glass, fashioning intricate mandala art. What began as a small and simple endeavor grew in complexity day by day.

As spring faded away with the changing seasons, something truly remarkable happened. Ms. Urashima's artistic creation began to transform before everyone's eyes. With scrupulous care, she expertly arranged each element, building layers upon layers that brought forth a sense of depth and intricacy in her masterpiece. And as the rainy season unfolded, the art took on a magical transformation, blossoming into a breathtaking three-dimensional marvel.

With grace and precision, Ms. Urashima's nimble fingers delicately positioned each individual rock, starting from the very core of the circle. Every piece found its rightful place, as if guided by an invisible hand. The result was a display that captivated all who beheld it, a testament to her talent and the love she poured into her craft.

The challenges brought forth by formidable typhoons attempted to disrupt the tranquility of the beach and the resilience of the natural art. But despite the onslaught of wind and rain, the masterpiece remained steadfast and unyielding. Its beauty and orderliness persevered, a testament to Ms. Urashima's unwavering dedication and the harmonious balance of nature itself.

Word of Ms. Urashima's captivating zen beach art spread like wildfire, gradually transforming the once-shabby fisherman's island into a vibrant and sought-after travel spot. It all started with a single visitor from Tokyo, whose heart was captured by the beauty of the intricate mandala. Unable to contain his excitement, he shared his experience with a friend, recounting the peaceful serenity that emanated from the art. Intrigued by the tale, the friend decided to embark on a journey to witness the artistry firsthand. Mesmerized by the impeccable three-dimensional mandala, they too became a storyteller, sharing their discovery with another friend. Like a chain reaction, whispers of the art's wonder continued spreading from one person to the next, until the entire island buzzed with anticipation and curiosity.

As the story spread, the island began to undergo a remarkable transformation. What was once a scruffy fishing community blossomed into a trendy, must-see travel location. The arrival of visitors inspired the emergence of new businesses. Ice cream shops enticed with their delectable treats, boba shops quenched the thirst of tourists, and souvenir stores offered tokens of the island's allure. A Yoga studio provided respite and tranquility, while an art gallery showcased the talents of local creatives. The island came alive with a vibrant energy, brimming with possibilities and hidden treasures.

Amidst the growing buzz, a local TV reporter seized the opportunity to interview the mayor, seeking answers about the enigmatic artistry that had captivated so many. "Who is the mastermind behind the incredible three-dimensional mandala art?" she inquired, her curiosity piqued. The mayor stumbled, his response carefully crafted. "The artist is a private individual, and I do not know her name. However, our island offers more than just her art. We have delectable cuisine, delightful ice cream, and a charming winery. Explore our stores and indulge in the full experience!" The reporter nodded, but the desire to unveil the artist's identity still burned within her.

Undeterred by the mayor's unhelpful response, the reporter continued her quest, determined to unearth the truth behind the incredible and sturdy nature mandala on the beach. While increasing visitors flocked to the island, enticed by the art and the vibrant atmosphere, the identity of the artist remained a well-guarded secret, shrouded in mystery.

Disheartened by the lack of leads, the reporter and her camera crew sought solace in the cozy confines of the nearby ice cream store. The place didn't only provide frozen treats; it had a cozy and inviting atmosphere that made conversations flow naturally and effortlessly. People gathered and chatted away without hesitation at any time of the day. Within its walls, a group of soccer moms met for their customary afternoon social gathering, indulging in double scoops of the ever-popular Lemon Lavender flavor.

As the sweet tang of the ice cream lingered on their tongues, the moms turned their conversation toward the mysterious artist behind the captivating beach art. A sense of intrigue mixed with trepidation danced in the air as they spoke. "She's a bit odd, don't you think?" mused one mom, a glimmer of admiration apparent in her voice. "But there's no denying her incredible artistic talent." Another mom, eager to share, chimed in, her eyes sparkling as she reminisced. "Oh, I was lucky enough to witness her in action. The way she meticulously arranged those rocks on the beach—it was like witnessing pure magic. And her son, he would always find the most exquisite rocks and pebbles for her creations."

Inukai, the intrepid reporter from TV *Daijobu* (It's All Good), couldn't resist the opportunity to delve deeper into the mystery. She approached the group, her voice filled with polite curiosity. "Excuse me, ladies. I couldn't help but overhear your conversation. I'm Inukai, a reporter for TV *Daijobu*. I'm actually here to report on the extraordinary beach art that remained intact even after the ferocious typhoon. Would any of you happen to know the artist responsible for such remarkable work?"

The moms exchanged glances, their expressions hesitant yet intrigued. One of them finally spoke up, her tone tinged with caution. "Well, I should warn you, she's quite an antisocial individual. She keeps to herself and rarely interacts with anyone besides her son." Inukai, undaunted by the warning, pressed on, her determination to uncover the truth burning bright within her. "I understand, but if you could just provide me with her name and perhaps a location where I can find her, it would be immensely helpful for my report."

The third mom pointed towards a weathered and worn cabin standing forlornly on the beach, its appearance a stark contrast to the bustling scene unfolding around it. "Urashima-san lives in that cabin over there," she revealed, a mixture of eagerness and reservation in her voice. With gratitude for the soccer moms' insight, Inukai and her camera crew bid them farewell, their minds swirling with anticipation and a hint of nervousness.

The house stood merely a four-minute walk away from the ice cream store. Inukai gazed at it, taking in the sight of the green house with its once pristine white trim. Memories of her time working at her father's architecture office came rushing back, reminding her of her knowledge about houses—both the well-cared-for and the neglected. As she assessed the structure of Urashima's house, she couldn't help but notice its underlying strength. Though the paint had peeled away, revealing a weathered exterior, the house seemed robust and ready for a fresh coat of paint. Inukai pondered why Urashima hadn't taken the initiative to repaint it.

Just then, a young boy dressed in a striped uniform made his way toward the house. Inukai saw an opportunity to make contact with

Urashima. Approaching the boy, she introduced herself with a friendly smile. "Hello there! My name is Inukai, and I'm a reporter from TV *Daijobu*. Could you kindly let Urashima-san know that I would like to speak with her? I believe she is your mom, right?"

The boy nodded, his eyes bright with wonder. "Sure," he responded, disappearing into the house. Inukai waited patiently, her anticipation growing. Within a matter of minutes, the boy, Taro, emerged from the house wearing a polite smile. "Please come in," he invited, his demeanor welcoming. Inukai followed Taro through the narrow hallway of the tiny, yet strangely intriguing cabin. Despite its size, the hallway seemed to stretch on endlessly, with two doors lining each side. Taro led Inukai and the camera crew towards the first door on the right, urging them to enter.

As the door swung open, a flood of bright, shimmering light greeted Inukai, enveloping her in a delightful embrace. The scent of the ocean filled the air, accompanied by the soothing sound of waves crashing against the shore. From deep within the room, a voice beckoned, "Welcome to the Summer Room."

Inukai was about to inquire if the voice belonged to Urashima-san, but her attention was swiftly diverted by the captivating scene before her. It wasn't just a room—it was as if a piece of untouched, natural beach had been transported indoors. The golden rays of sunlight cascaded down like drops of fresh lemon juice, while the transparent blue of the sky and sea seemed to merge seamlessly, creating a breathtaking three-dimensional painting. In that moment, Inukai found herself momentarily lost in the beauty of it all, forgetting the purpose of her visit. However, her focus shifted as she noticed the woman with the long black braid beckoning them forward.

"Let's start filming," Inukai exclaimed. "We're about to capture an incredible story." Simultaneously, Inukai's attention was drawn by the miraculous sight unfolding before her—hundreds of sea turtle eggs hatching. One by one, tiny hatchlings emerged, their struggle for survival both awe-inspiring and heartwarming. Inukai couldn't contain her astonishment. "This is amazing! How incredible!" she blurted, her words echoed by the stunned camera crew. Meanwhile, Taro hurriedly scurried towards the baby turtles, offering gentle encouragement to guide them towards the sea. With his help, each little hatchling found their way to the ocean. As if in harmony with their departure, a great wave crashed onto the shore, swallowing up the empty eggshells.

Then, to everyone's surprise, Taro boldly hopped onto the back of a large sea turtle, standing atop it like a skilled surfer on a board. With another powerful wave, Taro and the mother turtle disappeared into the depths of the sea. The woman with the long braid reassured them, "No worries, it's all part of the natural flow. Let's move on to the next room."

Inukai and her camera crew followed the woman with a sense of entrancement, their hearts filled with wonder as they ventured deeper into the cabin. Uncertain whether this woman was indeed Ms. Urashima, they yearned to uncover the truth. And lingering in their minds was the question of what had transpired with the boy in the Summer Room.

Slowly, the door across the hallway creaked open, revealing a space that was both dark and tranquil. The camera crew resumed filming, determined to capture whatever else would unfold before them. Though the room was notably cooler than the previous one, it held an undeniable sense of serenity. In the midst of a beautiful Japanese garden, their eyes were drawn to an altar adorned with a stack of dango, Japanese rice cakes, sitting atop an exquisite wooden tray. Above, the full moon glowed tenderly, casting a gentle radiance that illuminated the altar's intricate decorations.

The long braid woman pointed towards the miscanthus bushes, drawing their attention. In that moment, a white rabbit emerged, gracefully hopping out from the verdant foliage. The camera crew followed the rabbit's movements, only to be met with a disheartening realization. "Oh no! The battery is dead!" one of them exclaimed, frantically searching for a spare charger within their bag.

Meanwhile, the rabbit made another bound, landing effortlessly onto the long braid woman's outstretched hand. She gently rubbed the rabbit's velvety fur three times before tossing it into the air. Inukai's breath caught in her throat, and the camera crew's eyes lifted from the bag to the astonishing sight unfolding above them. The rabbit gracefully soared higher and higher, defying all logic as it ascended towards the moon. Inukai and her crew could hardly believe their eyes as the rabbit seemingly transformed into a solid figure, petrifying upon the moon itself. How was this possible? The moon, distant and unreachable, now bore the unmistakable shape of a rabbit, a sight that Inukai knew to be true.

Recovering from their shock, the long braid woman reassured them with a calm voice. "It's all part of the enchantment. Let us proceed to the next room," she said, leading the way with an air of confidence. As Inukai turned the doorknob, a sharp, icy coldness seeped into her hand, instantly alerting her to the fact that the next room was a wintry realm. The sensation hinted at the recent snowfall that had blanketed the area, transforming it into a serene winter wonderland. Delicate, powdery flakes continued to descend gracefully from the sky, creating a stunning scene before their eyes.

Inukai turned to her camera crew, and with urgency in her voice, she asked, "Did you put the new battery in the camera? We cannot afford to miss capturing this breathtaking sight." Aware of the importance of preserving the moment, she encouraged her team to ensure they were fully prepared.

Inside the room, the space was arranged to resemble a traditional Japanese temple. Along the left side stood a line of stone statues, known as *Jizo*. Each of their heads was adorned with a generous coating of snow, measuring around 15 centimeters tall. Observing the scene, the woman with the long braid approached one of the stone statues and gently brushed off the snow from its head. She then placed her own scarf atop it and joined her hands together in a prayerful gesture. Moving further into the temple hall, she discovered a pile of used towels. With care and reverence, she attended to each stone statue, meticulously removing the snow from their heads and providing them with the warmth of the discarded towels.

Inukai couldn't help but express her admiration. "That is incredibly generous and kind," she exclaimed, her voice filled with awe. The right side of the temple garden was adorned with numerous family graves, bearing the names of the departed. Undeterred by the snow, the long braid woman gracefully navigated through the winter landscape, knowing exactly where she was headed. She stopped where an ordinary gravestone stood bearing the name "Urashima Family's Resting Place."

Inukai turned to the long braid woman, her eyes filled with certainty. "You are the nature mandala artist, Urashima-san, aren't you?" she asked, seeking confirmation. With a solemn demeanor, the woman placed her hands together and bowed her head, choosing not to respond directly to Inukai's question. However, after a few moments, she shook off the snow from her head and offered a gentle smile in Inukai's direction. "It's all good, Inukai-san," she replied, her voice carrying a sense of reassurance. "Let us proceed to the last room, a place that remains unseen by others."

As Inukai stepped into the final room, a symphony of bird songs greeted her ears. "It must be spring!" she exclaimed, her voice filled with delight. However, in an instant, a powerful gust of wind rushed before her, swirling in a frenzy. It wasn't snow that danced in the air, but rather an awe-inspiring spectacle of millions of cherry blossom petals cascading around her. Inukai found herself immersed in a magnificent "Flower Blizzard," her eyes squinting as she attempted to discern the scene in front of her.

Through the flurry of petals, a vibrant picture emerged. She oversaw a children's soccer game unfolding on a field adorned with a carpet of colorful blossoms. Families stood on the sidelines, their voices lifted in cheers and encouragement for their little ones. Coaches passionately directed the young players, guiding them through the game. The soccer game brought Inukai back to her own childhood memories and made her feel nostalgic. She used to be one of those children darting across the field. Their energy and enthusiasm was infectious as they chased after the ball amidst the swirling petals of the flower blizzard.

Inukai's eyes followed the long braid woman as she walked towards the children's soccer game, directly towards the center of the wild pink petal storm. Inukai's arms, now submerged in a sea of petals, pushed forward, her determination driving her closer to the heart of the game. She called out, her voice carried away by the whimsical wind. "Urashima-san, are you the Zen Beach Artist? Wait up!" Her eyes scanned the field, searching for the elusive artist amidst the vibrant chaos.

As if guided by an invisible force, Inukai's gaze settled upon a figure standing amidst the flurry of blossoms. "Yes, I am the one who made the nature mandara art," the long braid woman revealed quietly. "I knew it!" Inukai screamed for joy. She had found the mysterious artist who had captured her imagination from the very beginning. With a skip in her step, Inukai approached Urashima-san, her heart brimming with excitement. This interview had the potential to become Inukai's career highlight, a moment she had eagerly awaited. The opportunity to explore Urashima-san's zen beach art, capturing its essence and unraveling its secrets, filled Inukai with a mixture of ambition and admiration.

But in the blink of a moment, "Whoosh!" Without warning, a large soccer ball hurtled towards Inukai and hit her face with tremendous force. "Crash!" The collision was swift and brutal, sending her sprawling to the ground. In the moments that followed, Inukai found herself in a daze, her consciousness wavering and her senses dulled by the overwhelming impact. A gentle voice whispered, "It's all good," before darkness claimed her.

Inukai awoke to find herself lying on the sandy beach. Her head throbbed with a dull ache and confusion washed over her as she tried to piece together the events that had led her there. With aching joints and a body that protested every movement, especially her knees, she struggled to rise. To her dismay, the camera crew was nowhere in sight. Questions swirled in her mind. "Where is Ms. Urashima? What had transpired after the unexpected blow?"

Summoning her strength, Inukai gathered herself and limped towards a nearby store, hoping to find some answers. "Hello," she began, her voice frail and hoarse, "My name is Inukai from TV *Daijobu*. Could you kindly let me borrow your phone?" The store owner wore an uneasy expression, but genuine concern filled his eyes as he responded, "Inukai? Are you alright? You look... well, awful." Inukai's gaze shifted to the showcase, where her reflection confirmed the store owner's observation. She had to admit that she appeared worse for wear. Grateful for the store owner's kindness, she accepted his offer of the phone and dialed the number of the TV *Daijobu* producer. The response she received left her reeling. "The number you dialed no longer exists." She tried again, disbelief coursing through her veins, only to be met with the same message.

Desperation clung to her as she stepped outside the store, the weight of uncertainty pressing upon her. "What is happening?" she whispered to the vast expanse of the beach, returning to the place where her journey had begun. She cast her gaze around, searching for any trace of the Zen Beach Art that had captivated her attention. "It should be here, intact despite the typhoon," she thought with conviction as her eyes scanned the shoreline for any sign of the art. It was then that she spotted an elderly man with a white beard strolling along the beach with his faithful canine companion.

Inukai approached the man, her voice trembling with a mix of hope and trepidation. "Excuse me," she began, "do you happen to know where the Zen Beach Art is on this beach?" The man regarded her with curiosity, his gaze lingering on her face before he responded, "And who might you be?" Inukai hesitated for a moment, before finding her voice once more. "My name is Inukai, from TV *Daijobu*. I am terribly confused. I only wanted to speak with Ms. Urashima about her art." The man's reply sent a chill down Inukai's spine. "I'm not quite sure what you're referring to, but I have heard tales of an incredible zen beach art piece that was relocated to a museum several decades ago."

The realization hit Inukai like a tidal wave crashing upon the shore. "That's it! The person behind that masterpiece was Ms. Urashima! But wait... Didn't she already admit it?" she said, her voice filled with a mix of excitement and despair, trying to understand. But the man's mention of the art's relocation several decades ago shattered her hopes. "What does that mean?" she whispered, her knees giving way beneath her. "I'm sorry," the man offered, his expression filled with sincere sympathy. Unsure of how to provide solace in the face of Inukai's distress, he departed with his dog, "Let's go, Pochi," leaving Inukai to grapple with her overwhelming emotions and unanswered queries.

Venturing further along the beach, Inukai's weary steps led her to the ramshackle cabin adorned in faded green hues with a hint of whitish trim. It was Urashima's house, or so she believed. However, to her astonishment, a sign on the front door read, "Inukai." Confusion etched across her face as she questioned, "Is this my house?"

Summoning every ounce of her remaining strength, Inukai reached out to grasp the doorknob. A peculiar sensation coursed through her hand, a sharp jolt that crackled like lightning. In that very instant, something extraordinary occurred. Inukai felt herself shrinking, her body diminishing to two-thirds the size of her former stature, her back now stooped with age. She turned her eyes towards a nearby window, desperately trying to make sense of the unimaginable. As her reflection appeared, the truth was laid bare before her aging eyes. Inukai, once vibrant and youthful, now stood before her reflection as a centenarian. The weight of a century's worth of experiences and the relentless passage of time had taken hold, leaving her astonished by this unexpected twist of fate. The reality of her newfound age, in such stark contrast to her former self, left her bewildered and grappling with a whirlwind of unsettling emotions.

Inukai's mind was foggy but it still reeled with the conviction of the unimaginable. "This was Urashima's curse!" she uttered in disbelief, her voice barely a whisper. The weight of the revelation settled upon her, the realization that she had unknowingly. It appeared she had traveled forward in time quite significantly; judging by her appearance, it looked to be at least 70 years or more! It felt unfathomable, like a tale that nobody would truly comprehend.

As she sat there, her mind in a state of utter confusion, a familiar green minivan rolled up in front of the house, offering a glimmer of hope in that fleeting moment. Inukai's heart leapt with anticipation, hoping it was TV *Daijobu* coming to her rescue. However, her excitement quickly turned to disappointment as she realized that it was not what she hoped for after all. Stepping out from the van was the long-braid woman, carrying an empty wheelchair.

“Urashima san...!” As Inukai’s desperate voice faded, the long-braid woman just smiled peacefully. With utmost care, she guided the empty chair to Inukai's side.

"Hello, Ms. Inukai," the long-braid woman greeted her with a serene smile. "Thank you for waiting for me for a long time. I will assist you into this chair. Don’t worry, *Daijobu*, it's all good." With gentle hands, she lifted Inukai from her bewildered state and carefully settled her into the wheelchair. Inukai's consciousness began to fade, much like the memory of the young boy riding on the turtle into the embrace of the crashing waves. His name slipped from her mind, lost in the haze of time.

In a drowsy state, Inukai murmured those comforting words that had echoed throughout her journey. "*Daijobu*, it's all good now," she repeated, finding solace in their reassurance. Slowly, she succumbed to sleep, nestled in the wheelchair that now cradled her aging form.

At the beach, a bunch of sandpipers darted down and made sudden turns just before reaching the beach house, as if the house was a sacred structure that nobody was allowed to touch.

Medetashi, medetashi. Happily Ever After.

6

Reverence

It begins with reverence and ends with reverence. ~Japanese Proverb

Kintaro Strong Boy

Once upon a time, in the bustling metropolis of Northern Tokyo, lived Ojii-san and Obaa-san, a charming elderly couple with no little ones to call their own. Their humble abode was nestled snugly in a conservative apartment that had seen its fair share of decades pass by, just like the couple themselves.

Now, Ojii-san was a seasoned veteran of a prestigious Japanese bank, eagerly awaiting his well-deserved retirement in a mere three years. Alas, life has a funny way of pulling the rug from under our feet when we least expect it. One particular day, as Ojii-san arrived at his office, he was confronted with unthinkable news—the bank, regrettably, had decided to declare bankruptcy. This unexpected turn of events left its loyal employees, including Ojii-san, in quite a financial pickle.

Forty years of dedicated service, and what did he have to show for it? Not a single yen from his hard-earned retirement savings and pensions. As the news of the company's collapse reached his ears, Ojii-san's shoulders slumped, matching the somber hue of his gray suits. With this news weighing on his heart, he could do nothing but set out on his usual subway journey from *Akihabara* station back to home.

The morning rush had subsided, and the train was relatively empty by this time of the day. Yet, luck seemed to have taken the day off, for there wasn't an empty seat in sight for the weary Ojii-san. Young folks, oblivious to his presence, comfortably occupied the available seats. Their hoods were pulled up, shielding them from the world, their attention glued to the mesmerizing screens of their smartphones in front of them.

Now, Ojii-san had every right to harbor some negative feelings toward these self-absorbed youths. However, the burden of worrying about tomorrow weighed far more heavily on his shoulders than the ignorant passengers occupying the seats. After all, the future holds far more possibilities than a momentary frustration with the younger generation, right? "What am I going to do?" Ojii-san pondered, his gaze fixed on the buildings and apartments rushing past the subway window. The weight of uncertainty hung heavily in the air as he searched for answers amidst the midday city sights.

Meanwhile, Obaa-san had embarked on her own little adventure to the dry cleaning store, tasked with retrieving Ojii-san's impeccably pressed suits. As she eagerly awaited his impending retirement in a mere three years, her thoughts took a whimsical turn.

"In just a short while, he'll bid farewell to this place, and I won't have to make these trips anymore," Obaa-san whispered to herself, a mischievous glimmer lighting up her eyes. The tantalizing prospect of freedom and adventure swirled in her mind, as she envisioned grand explorations of Japan's renowned hot springs alongside her beloved husband.

But before heading back home, Obaa-san's senses pulled her off course as she was captivated by the irresistible aroma wafting from a nearby meat vendor. The temptation of a scrumptious dinner became impossible to ignore. Yielding to her cravings, she made a delightful decision: she would treat Ojii-san and herself to four golden croquettes, each hiding a delectable surprise of creamy, mashed potatoes inside.

With dinner supplies in hand and a satisfied smirk on her face, Obaa-san continued on her way, strolling past a charming little park nestled in the corner. However, her keen eyes caught sight of something unusual. A treasure box, seemingly out of place, radiated a mesmerizing glow, captivating her inquisitive nature. It called out to her with an air of enchantment, beckoning her to explore its secret.

"Well, well, well! What do we have here?" Obaa-san's mind spun with anticipation. Unable to resist the allure, she cautiously approached the box, ensuring no prying eyes were watching her. With a mixture of thrill and dare, she delicately cradled the treasure box, as though holding a long-lost secret, and sneakily carried it home. When Obaa-san returned home, she unexpectedly found Ojii-san already there, diligently preparing hot water for their evening tea.

"*Okaeri,* welcome home, Obaa-san," Ojii-san greeted her with a warm smile. "*Tadaima*, I am home, Ojii-san. You're early today," Obaa-san remarked, a hint of surprise in her voice. Without wasting a moment, she excitedly blurted out, "Look at what I found in the kids' park!"

Before she could even finish her sentence, Ojii-san's eyes widened in amazement, captivated by the shimmering beam streaming through the crack in the treasure box. With a look of concern on his face, Ojii-san nervously exclaimed, "Obaa-san, it might be dangerous. We should take it to the police!" But Obaa-san, ever the adventurous spirit, persisted, "Chill, Ojii-san. Let's open it first." Her curiosity simply couldn't be contained. And so, with a mix of caution and anticipation, they opened the mysterious box. And what awaited them inside was beyond their wildest imagination—a newborn baby boy!

"Oh, my goodness! It's a baby boy!" Obaa-san exclaimed, her heart brimming with joy. "We finally got our baby!" Ojii-san and Obaa-san couldn't contain their excitement as they gently lifted the precious bundle from the box. But their joy was quickly met with surprise and concern when the baby stretched his little arms and promptly rolled onto the floor. "Obaa-san, you have to be careful," Ojii-san cautioned, a touch of frustration in his voice. "But Ojii-san, look! The baby is growing!" Obaa-san exclaimed, as if they were witnessing a scene straight out of a sci-fi movie. Each time the baby stretched, he seemed to grow larger and larger before their eyes.

In a matter of minutes, the baby had transformed into a fully clothed teenage boy. With a cheerful smile, he introduced himself, saying, "Hi, Ojii-san and Obaa-san. My name is Kintaro. Can I live with you?" Ojii-san and Obaa-san stood there, their jaws dropped in disbelief. They exchanged bewildered glances, waiting for each other's reaction. Ojii-san's smile faded, and he hesitantly murmured, "I don't think we can..." But Obaa-san, always quick to embrace the unexpected, interrupted him, "Why not?"

Ojii-san's expression turned somber as he shared the unfortunate news, "My company went bankrupt. I have no job or retirement funds." Obaa-san couldn't believe what she had just heard from her husband. "Oh, no, Ojii-san! That's terrible. What are we going to do?" Kintaro interjected, interrupting their conversation. "Ojii-san, Obaa-san, I am going to win the Strong Man contest in just two weeks. The grand prize is a whopping ten billion yen!"

Ojii-san and Obaa-san were dumbfounded, their minds reeling with disbelief. How could they possibly trust this peculiar teenager to achieve such a remarkable feat? Before they could voice their concerns, Obaa-san chimed in with unwavering faith, "This boy is a miracle from a magic box. He can make miracles happen. I trust him! By the way, why don't we have dinner? I am hungry, are you?"

Determined to show her support, Obaa-san swiftly made her way to the kitchen, skillfully preparing a delightful spread. She served steaming bowls of rice, fragrant tofu and *wakame* (seaweed) *miso* (bean paste) soup, two delicious croquettes, and a plate of thinly sliced cabbage for Kintaro. Ojii-san and Obaa-san were content with just one croquette, as it was more than enough for their appetites. The three of them settled around a low dining table, seated on a *tatami* mat, and savored the flavors of the meal while relishing in each other's company.

With no pressing obligations following his job loss, Ojii-san found a new purpose in helping train Kintaro for the Strong Man contest. As memories resurfaced of his glory days on the high-school track team, specializing in the discus and earning numerous medals, Ojii-san felt a renewed vigor within him. The magic treasure box provided everything they needed for Kintaro and Ojii-san's training endeavors. Whenever they required training clothes, the box magically produced them—shoes, fresh underwear, socks, weights, dumbbells, jump ropes—everything Kintaro needed appeared at their fingertips. And as soon as they finished using the items, they would simply place them back in the box, where they would disappear, leaving no need for additional storage space.

Obaa-san, always the thoughtful caretaker, prepared three generous rice balls—two for Kintaro and one for Ojii-san. As the days passed, Ojii-san grew stronger with each workout session. Drawing from his own experience, he taught Kintaro the art of soothing exhausted muscles through massage. Without fail, every day was dedicated to relentless training, with Ojii-san and Kintaro pushing themselves to the limit. Obaa-san even joined in for light jogs, her presence adding a cheerful touch to their daily routines.

Night after night, the trio gathered around the dining table and enjoyed their nourishing meals together. And where did the food come from? You guessed it—straight from the magic treasure box itself. It seemed that not only had Kintaro entered their lives as a miraculous presence, but the box itself had become an endless source of sustenance and support, catering to their every need.

The day of the Strong Man Contest had finally arrived, and Kintaro stood tall and confident, ready to face his fellow competitors. Ojii-san, Obaa-san, and Kintaro were in excellent condition, their training paying off in leaps and bounds. Retirement worries were a thing of the past for Ojii-san and Obaa-san, as their faith in Kintaro's abilities soared.

The trio left home bright and early, jogging two stations away from their humble apartment and setting out two stations before reaching the competition venue, determined to squeeze in some extra exercise. With each step, their anticipation grew, fueled by the unwavering belief that Kintaro would emerge victorious in this championship.

The first round focused on basic strength. Judges meticulously measured the muscle mass of each competitor, conducted tests to detect any use of prohibited substances, challenged their nutritional knowledge, and even evaluated their heart strength through EKG readings. Kintaro breezed through every test with ease, impressing the judges and solidifying his position as a formidable contender.

In the second round, the intensity reached new heights. An obstacle course awaited the competitors; here they would showcase their strength in three distinct ways. Kintaro approached the first challenge—a massive boulder. With remarkable agility, he swiftly climbed up and then descended, effortlessly pushing the boulder back to the start line. While his competitors may have matched his strength, they sorely lacked Kintaro's agility, leaving them trailing behind.

Next in line was the daunting obstacle of a large red *Toyota* Tacoma truck. Kintaro devised a clever strategy, wrapping a sturdy metal chain around the vehicle. Positioning himself in front of the truck, his teeth glistened, strengthened by his daily intake of fish, milk, and Obaa-san's nutritious rice balls. With determination etched on his face, Kintaro clenched the chain with his teeth, emitting a resounding "Aaaaa!" He began pulling the colossal truck with sheer force, surprising both the spectators and his fellow competitors. While others were still struggling to secure their own chains, Kintaro gained momentum, inch by inch, until the Toyota Tacoma started to budge. With a burst of energy, he summoned his might and, in one mighty pull, propelled the truck to the top of the hill.

Atop the hill awaited another challenge—ten 100-kilogram iron balls. The contestants were tasked with loading all the balls into the truck and pushing it across the finish line. Obaa-san shook her pom-poms enthusiastically, rallying support with her spirited cheers of "Let's go, Kintaro!" Ojii-san, too, joined in, exclaiming proudly, "That's my son! Go, Kintaro!" The announcers couldn't contain their excitement as they reported each of Kintaro's awe-inspiring moves. The audience erupted in a chorus of cheers, chanting "Kintaro, Kintaro!" with fervor. When Kintaro's Toyota Tacoma finally crossed the finish line, the entire arena erupted in thunderous applause, celebrating the most remarkable strongman they had ever witnessed before.

But the competition was far from over. The final challenge awaited, ready to test Kintaro's resilience, proving that he truly deserved the coveted title of the Strong Man Contest champion.

The final task presented a daunting challenge—moving ten semi-truck tires from one side to the other. Competitors had the option to carry one tire at a time or attempt multiple tires simultaneously. Not discouraged by the enormity of the task, Kintaro, summoning his miraculous speed, piled all ten tires on top of one another, planning to push the stack across the finish line.

As Kintaro began exerting his tremendous strength, the audience erupted once again, their cheers echoing throughout the arena. Even the announcers, former champions themselves, couldn't believe their eyes. Ten tires, carefully balanced, moved inch by inch under Kintaro's unwavering determination. His face reddened, and sweat poured down his brow, arms, back, and every other inch of his being, creating a radiant sheen on his skin.

Finally, amidst the deafening applause and the burst of confetti, Kintaro triumphantly crossed the final finish line, his feat a testament to his indomitable spirit and unmatched strength. He was acclaimed as the ten billion yen Strong Man Contest Winner! A reporter with shimmering coal black hair eagerly approached Kintaro, thrusting her microphone forward. "Congratulations, Kintaro! What are you planning to do with your prize?"

Still catching his breath, Kintaro beamed with pride as he responded, "This is retirement money for my father and mother." His selfless gesture touched the hearts of those watching, inspiring admiration for his character as well as his strength.

News of Kintaro's victory spread like wildfire. The moment was captured on TV and quickly shared across social media platforms. The hashtag #Kintaro gained traction, garnering an impressive following of twelve million fans on his Instagram and viewed by one hundred million people on Tiktok. Recognizing his potential, Nike reached out to Kintaro and offered to sponsor him for further training. Additionally, a prominent protein bar company approached him, eager to feature him in their commercial.

Media attention opened up new income opportunities for Ojii-san and Obaa-san, who were immensely grateful for the positive impact Kintaro had brought to their lives. No longer ordinary Ojii-san and Obaa-san, they had transformed into strong and healthy seniors through Kintaro's dedicated training and unwavering support.

After the exhilarating Strong Man Contest, Ojii-san, Obaa-san, and Kintaro continued their commitment to fitness and wellness. One day, as they reflected on their incredible journey, Ojii-san proposed a heartfelt idea. "Why don't we share our experiences and give back our extensive knowledge of wellness to the community?"

Instead of just purchasing a plot of land, Ojii-san, Obaa-san, and Kintaro decided to acquire a sizable building for their community initiatives. With their substantial resources, they aimed to create a comprehensive center that could accommodate various programs and services. The vision was to establish a thriving hub where individuals of all ages and backgrounds could gather, engage in physical activities, receive financial guidance, access educational resources, and foster a strong sense of community. By providing a wide range of services, they aimed to address the diverse needs of their community members.

Within the new building, Ojii-san dedicated his expertise to offering free financial consultations to those who couldn't afford a professional advisor. His selfless guidance provided much-needed support to individuals striving for financial stability. Meanwhile, Obaa-san, with the help of dedicated volunteers, channeled her culinary talents into making nutritious rice balls for homeless individuals, extending a helping hand through a warm meal.

Kintaro, now recognized as a seasoned fitness advisor, assumed the role of lead trainer in the community gym. His passion for health and wellness ignited a spark in those who joined him, motivating them to push their limits and achieve their own personal fitness goals.

The new community building became a beacon of hope and support, offering its services entirely free of charge. One might assume that the ten billion yen prize would quickly diminish, but they would be mistaken. Ojii-san, drawing from his 40 years of financial experience, made wise investments. Half of the prize money was strategically allocated to prominent AI technology and some start-up machine learning companies, resulting in a remarkable tripling of its initial value.

Meanwhile, Obaa-san's delectable rice balls garnered attention from Japanese cooking shows and celebrity chef magazines. Her talent and unique spin on traditional recipes caught the public's eye, propelling her into the role of an esteemed author. Her Rice Ball Recipe book skyrocketed to the top of the New York Times bestseller list, remaining there for an impressive fourteen consecutive weeks.

Through their combined efforts, Ojii-san, Obaa-san, and Kintaro not only made a positive impact on their own lives but also transformed the lives of countless others within their community.

Ojii-san, Obaa-san, and Kintaro continued to live humbly in their beloved apartment until the day Kintaro found love and decided to get married. In their ever-growing love and respect for family, they embarked on a new project—a humble yet spacious house that could accommodate two generations on the premises of their community gym property. This way, they could always remain close and continue to strengthen and cherish their bond.

The magic treasure box remained a cherished part of their lives. Whenever Ojii-san and Obaa-san opened it, they found an abundance of supplies that met their immediate needs. It seemed as though the box itself had an endless capacity to provide for them, reinforcing the belief that life had indeed rewarded them with remarkable blessings.

In their new home, surrounded by loved ones and the shared values they held dear, Ojii-san, Obaa-san, and Kintaro embraced a lifetime of happiness and contentment. They created a legacy of love, compassion, and generosity, touching the lives of those around them and leaving an indelible mark on their community.

Medetashi, medetashi. Happily Ever After.

7

The Mysterious Moon

Clouds gather around the moon.
~Japanese Proverb

K*aguya Hime* Shining Princess

Once upon a time, childless Ojii-san (Old Man) and Obaa-san (Old Woman) lived in a small village in Southern Japan. They had been fortunate to live in a decent house that they inherited from Obaa-san's family. The couple worked as farmers growing and selling small amounts of healthy vegetables like spinach, Chinese cabbage, daikon radish, cucumbers, green tea leaves, *shiso* leaves, shiitake mushrooms, and bamboo shoots. They had previously owned rice field patches in the area, however, they decided to give that up in order to reduce the physical burden of farming as they aged... well, not completely.

The couple didn't have any children on their own, but they loved young kids. Ojii-san and Obaa-san enjoyed being surprised by the neighborhood's young children's unexpected verbal expressions and intriguing points of views in their frequent interactions. As a result, the idea came pretty naturally to them. Ojii-san and Obaa-san proposed a children's hands-on farming experiences program to the nearby school district when they decided to retire from the rice field work. It would allow them to have more time with kids to fulfill the rest of their lives while also making more room to volunteer in their community. Instead of working by themselves, the old couple offered to teach young students how to grow and harvest rice so all the labor could be done by school children and staff. At harvest time, all the rice could provide school lunch for the children. It was a win-win for the school and the couple.

Ojii-san and Obaa-san enjoyed working with the kids, from rambunctious pre-schoolers to sassy high schoolers. Especially on humid and scorching hot June days, which were often rainy, children enjoyed planting the young green rice plants in the muddy fields. Along with planting little rice plants, Ojii-san's plan prepared for the children's expected naughtiness. Ojii-san enjoyed watching the kids get mud on their faces, chase after frogs, giggle at a classmate's leg being bitten by leeches, and throw mud to get each other's attention. After planting sessions were over, all the kids lined up in a single file, and Ojii-san sprayed them down with the hose, one by one, to clean their bodies. Their joyous screaming and laughter lasted for a long time until Obaa-san brought onigiri rice balls for the children and teachers. Their wet clothes dried very quickly in the intense summer heat. Everyone was full of contentment and joy. Ojii-san and Obaa-san's hearts were complete in moments like this. No matter how hot or wet the weather was, everyone always had a blast during the summer rice planting time.

One night, Ojii-san sighed peacefully and blurted at the dinner table, “Kids are fun to work with. I wish we could have our own, don’t you, Obaa-san?” Obaa-san nodded, “I know, it’s too unfortunate and too late for us to have our own, but let’s be thankful for our time with the young children in the farming program.”

The Rice Farming Program had been successful for three years in a row, and it grew stronger each year. Even graduates visited to help during busy planting and harvesting time. Ojii-san and Obaa-san celebrated their success and felt grateful for the privilege to serve their community. Ojii-san and Obaa-san’s agricultural program gradually expanded to include everything from planting rice fields to tending vegetable gardens, harvesting oranges to cultivating tea leaves, and even digging for bamboo shoots.

One spring day after a rainstorm, Ojii-san and Obaa-san went on their first bamboo shoot digging trip of the season. The rain had softened the soil for the old couple to dig the shoots up easier. Digging for a bamboo shoot was, unlike harvesting other vegetables, tricky. They had to dig around a bamboo shoot very deep in order to pull it up with the whole beautiful large rocket ship shape still intact. But it was easy for the hoe to hurt the bamboo shoot’s body if they weren’t careful. Once they were able to create a nice space around the bamboo shoot, they could use the lever principle to push it up and out.

Although it was physically tough work, Obaa-san giggled with joy each time she found the bamboo shoot’s pointy head sticking up above the ground. The couple’s first day was extremely successful with three large bamboo shoots. The rest of the bamboo shoots could be available for the farming program later in the week. "Are we ready to go home, Obaa-san?" Ojii-san asked her lovingly. "It sounds good to me," Obaa-san answered.

As they stood up from their squatting position, a bright shiny light straight up from the ground to the sky like a spotlight caught Obaa-san's eye. "Look, Ojii-san!" Obaa-san pointed her finger to the mysterious bright light. "Oh my goodness, that is so bright! What is it? Is it from a bamboo shoot?" Ojii-san and Oba-san gingerly approached the source of the magical bright light.

A new bamboo shoot's head was poking out from the ground which was exactly where the bright light was coming from. The couple looked at each other and nodded speechlessly. Then they began to dig around the mysteriously shiny bamboo shoot in the usual way, but extra carefully.

"There!" With all of his strength, Ojii-san successfully pulled up the bright bamboo shoot. He handed it to Obaa-san who started peeling the skin one layer at a time. After the first couple layers of skin were removed, Ojii-san and Obaa-san gasped.

"Do you see what I see?" Obaa-san asked Ojii-san. Before Ojii-san answered the question, IT cried! "Waaa, Waaa!" It was not a bamboo shoot, but a baby GIRL! "Obaa-san, we have a baby!" Ojii-san couldn't hide his joy. They had been wanting their own baby for so long. Obaa-san held the baby in her arms and looked at her with an adoring gaze. "She is our shiny princess. So let's call her *Kaguya Hime* (he-mei)," she said. This excitement made them forget all about the three bamboo shoots that they had dug up previously. They left for their sweet home with their newborn baby girl quite excitedly, leaving the three newly dug bamboo shoots behind them.

Next morning, Kaguya Hime greeted them with her brightest smile, "Good morning, Ojii-san, Obaa-san." Kaguya Hime was no longer an infant, but appeared to be a two-year-old toddler in a red silk *kimono* dress! The couple didn't seem to care how Kaguya Hime had transformed overnight. Obaa-san lovingly hugged her and said, "You woke up so early, Kaguya Hime. How cute you are!"

Kaguya Hime followed Obaa-san on her little busy feet everywhere she went while Ojii-san did other house chores. Obaa-san patiently taught Kaguya Hime about each household item and how to use them. When she folded a towel in the finished laundry, Obaa-san cheered her. While Ojii-san went to pick up yesterday's three bamboo shoots by himself, Obaa-san taught their toddler simple Origami tricks in addition to the easy house chores. Every day, the little princess learned as much as she could like a sponge. Of course, her parents often took her out to the field and bamboo hills, too, telling Kaguya Hime how magical the day was when they found her.

By the seventh day, Kaguya Hime had grown to approximately four years old. She was eager to learn more and curious about everything she saw. Ojii-san and Obaa-san taught her how to count potatoes, add and subtract money, read books, and write letters in Japanese calligraphy. The couple took her to the local Elementary School's Rice Field and extended agriculture Education classes, and Kaguya Hime helped her parents as a kid assistant. But don't underestimate this "kid" assistant. She calculated how many rice plants could be planted in each row of a rice field patch before Ojii-san figured it out on the paper. These educational experiences were fun but they didn't satisfy Kaguya Hime.

"Ojii-san, Obaa-san, I want to go to school," Kaguya Hime asked. "Great idea! We want you to learn everything you want to know in this world!" Ojii-san answered. "Only one problem is that we don't know how quickly you will age. You could be a teenager by next week," Obaa-san worried. So they decided to enroll her in high school the following week.

Kaguya Hime, on the verge of turning fifteen, found herself standing at the threshold of a brand-new chapter in her life. She had enrolled in a private girls' high school, the only option available to her, as it was the sole institution open to admitting new students in the middle of the academic year. With an unwavering spirit, Kaguya Hime's determination blazed inside her like an unstoppable fire. She embarked on a daring mission, a week-long marathon where she devoured every textbook in sight—yes, you heard that right, an entire week!

But she didn't stop there. Oh no, not our determined Kaguya Hime. Driven by her insatiable thirst for knowledge, she fearlessly approached her teachers with a bold request—to participate in the very same end-of-year tests reserved for only the experienced students. Now, let me tell you, in the realm of Japanese academia, the system was rigid, bound by tradition, and offered little room for exceptions. However, Kaguya Hime's peers and educators were well aware of her unparalleled talent, her intellectual capability, and her unstoppable desire to expand her mind. Thus, against all odds, her request received not only recognition but also approval, all the way up to the esteemed office of the principal.

Before *OBON*, that magical time in mid-August when ancestral spirits come to visit, Kaguya Hime's mind was buzzing with possibilities. She had her eyes on a few universities that offered programs in Artificial Intelligence. Her dream? To create an AI that thought and behaved like a human, but with a special twist. This AI would become a farmer's ultimate companion, providing them with all the up-to-date data they needed.

Imagine this: farmers working hand in hand with an AI that knows all the ins and outs of their land. It would help them design the most efficient farmland layout, taking into account every little detail. But it wouldn't stop there. This super-smart AI would also be able to analyze weather patterns, giving farmers invaluable insights for their crop choices. It would even calculate the right amount of fertilizer to use, making sure nothing went to waste. And if that wasn't enough, it would predict how many hours of work were needed, making sure everyone's time was put to good use. Plus, it would come up with healthy meal plans for the hardworking laborers and take care of all the boring bookkeeping. And on top of all that, it would have user-friendly tools for self-care. Talk about a dream come true!

Kaguya Hime couldn't be more grateful for the love and support she had received from Ojii-san and Obaa-san. They had always been there for her, going above and beyond what was expected of them. She wanted to show her appreciation by doing something equally meaningful. That's why combining her smarts with her parents' passion for farming felt like the perfect match. And let's not forget, AI farming wasn't just about her parents—it had the potential to change the lives of farmers everywhere!

Before submitting college applications, Kaguya-Hime started to receive calls and letters from numerous prestigious colleges, not only in Japan, but all over the world. No one could determine how all those schools had learned of her and her talent. Ojii-san and Obaa-san became so overwhelmed with such a number of fine offers in just one day. Ojii-san said, "Kaguya Hime, you are so lucky! I am so proud of you. Just pick whatever school you like the best!" Obaa-san also excitedly added, "Your future's so bright no matter which college you attend!" They were too excited to notice their daughter's concerned eyes.

The first school official invited Kaguya Hime's family to their campus. Officials took the family on a campus tour, which showcased a beautifully modernized computer science building, multiple libraries, student center, student dorms, the library, the student dining halls, etc. They showed the latest technology students could access. Obaa-san thought this was the best fit for her daughter. Kaguya Hime politely talked to the officials, sharing, "Your school has the latest technology we could never dream of. But your school doesn't have an athletic center nor large fields for students to exercise. Physical movement is essential for the best learning performance and outcomes. I don't think I can utilize my full potential on this campus. I appreciate your offer, however, I must decline." Ojii-san and Obaa-san were in shock but they understood what their daughter had told the school. So they left.

The next school official visited Ojii-san and Obaa-san's personal residence. Obaa-san smiled at them, "*Irasshaimase.* Welcome, it is a small place, but please be comfortable." Ojii-san offered zabuton cushions to the officials. On one side, three officials sat on the zabuton cushions, and Kaguya Hime's family sat on the other side. One of the officials brought a box in a *furoshiki,* the traditional wrapping cloth. He began to talk, "I heard you have successful hands-on agricultural education for youth in your community. It sounds very exciting and admirable. We thought this might support your program." Then, he unwrapped the *furoshiki* wrapping cloth and exposed what was inside.

"Oh, gosh, it's unbelievable!" Obaa-san gasped. Inside the *furoshiki* wrapping cloth was... at least ten piles of 10,000 yen bills. Ojii-san was immediately enraged, as indicated by the red blood streaks in his eyes. He sharply but calmly declared, "Do you know what you are doing? I don't feel comfortable sending our daughter to your school. Please leave our property. Now!" So they did.

Obaa-san put her hands on Ojii-san's shoulders. "Parenting is harder than what we expected. How could we imagine something like this would happen? But thank you for standing up for our daughter. What are we going to do?" Obaa-san sighed. "I know, I know. No worries, eventually, we will find the best school for Kaguya Hime," Ojii-san replied discouragingly. And this time, too, they were too exhausted to notice sadness in Kaguya Hime's eyes. She was staring at the moon shining a million miles away from home.

Not long after, another school official was about to schedule a meeting with the family on their campus when Kaguya Hime pulled her mother's sleeve hesitantly. "Obaa-san, I need to talk to you about something really important," Kaguya Hime spoke with a sense of urgency, her voice carrying a weight that demanded attention. "What's going on?" Ojii-san's concern drew him closer, his presence a pillar of support. The three of them formed a tight circle in the living room, creating a space where they could share and listen.

Taking a deep breath, Kaguya Hime mustered the courage to speak her truth. Her words were filled with gratitude and love, but they also carried a tinge of difficulty. "First and foremost, Ojii-san and Obaa-san, I want to thank you for raising me, protecting me, and loving me unconditionally. I love you both so much. There's something I've been meaning to tell you, but it's been really hard for me to find the words.

“It hasn't been easy for me to gather the courage to bring up this matter, but... I come from the moon. The Moon Tribe sent me here on a significant mission. NASA and other space projects haven’t even identified the Moon Tribe that is conducting fascinating research on artificial human models like myself, which studies how closely we can replicate the physical and emotional behaviors of real humans.

“I'm humbled to share that I have exceeded their expectations in terms of my physical development and intelligence. It's a testament to the advanced technology of the Moon Tribe. Now their vision expands further. They are looking to develop more AI models like me, not only in human form but also in various other applications. This includes industrial materials, medical equipment, and even farming products. They strive to create a sustainable food supply for the moon's climate without relying on traditional farming methods before the humans migrate to the moon.”

Ojii-san interrupted, “Wait, why does the Moon Tribe want to develop all those artificial things?” “Because,” Kaguya Hime sadly looked at him, “We know the earth is aging. The earth is not going to be a healthy planet forever, unfortunately.” “What does it mean?” Obaa-san asked. “The Moon Tribe has a project underway to create a new environment on the moon for the people of earth. When this project is complete, humans would be able to live on the moon without space suits. And it is nearly done." Kaguya Hime answered determinedly.

Kaguya Hime continued, "The Moon Tribe didn't predict one thing accurately, though. That was... how fast the earth was aging.

"Humans must face consequences sooner than we predicted. Consciously and unconsciously, the earth has been brutally harmed. The damage is non-curable. There is no time to argue about whether global warming is true or not. We have to take action, NOW!"

Kaguya Hime was visibly upset although her voice remained calm. Obaa-san wrapped her arms around her daughter and whispered, "Child, breathe. We understand you are frustrated about how slow our actions are to help the aging earth. But what could we do? What can you do?"

"Ojii-san, Obaa-san, we don't have time to discuss, but we have to migrate to the moon by the next full moon." "That is just two weeks from now," Ojii-san mumbled. "Let's all go to the moon together on the 15th!" Kaguya-Hime suggested. "I must save you from the dying earth. Please come with me," Kaguya Hime pleaded. "Kaguya Hime... I am so proud of you, but I can't leave here," Ojii-san said. "I was born and raised here on earth. The earth has been providing rice fields, bamboo hills, and vegetable gardens to support our lives. If the earth is dying, it needs me! I can't leave here knowing that the earth is in such terrible condition. We must stand up and save our earth!"

Kaguya Hime realized that she couldn't change Ojii-san's firm determination. "Ojii-san, I hear and respect your wishes. And I will support you however I can until the next full moon," Kaguya Hime said.

Following that conversation, Ojii-san, Obaa-san, and Kaguya Hime became busier than ever taking care of the vegetable garden and supporting the Youth Agricultural Education Project for hundreds of children. In the meantime, Kaguya Hime invented a phone app that controls water supplies and fertilizer. This app was simultaneously controlled from the home computer. She also developed an innovative school lunch app that designed a nutritionally appropriate menu using fresh produce from Ojii-san and Obaa-san's property and other local farmers'. The program analyzed and predicted the co-relationship between students' learning productivity based on the different nutritional needs and amounts they consumed.

The next full moon day arrived. Ojii-san and Obaa-san protected Kaguya Hime inside of the house so no one could come to get her. They selected thirty armed bodyguards wearing a suit and sunglasses to stand around the house. These warriors were not only physically strong, but also highly intelligent, knowing the Moon Tribe might attack in cyberspace. They strategized to save Kaguya Hime from the Moon Tribe, however they might approach their house.

As the moon rose above the mountain top, the brightest moonlight beamed on Kaguya Hime like a spotlight through the window. "It's time," Kaguya Hime whispered to herself. She squeezed Oji-san and Obaa-san's hands tightly. Then she released their hands graciously and hugged them one at a time. "I love you and I will never forget about your love," Kaguya Hime said. "I wish I could live with you forever." Obaa-san cried, "Kaguya Hime, thirty guards should be able to protect you. I don't want you to go."

Before Obaa-san could finish her sentence, Kaguya Hime swiftly rose to her feet, extending her arms gracefully towards the sky. In one fluid motion, she bent her body, moving like a serene yoga practitioner. Then, like a gentle metamorphosis, her body curled into a ball as she assumed the position known as the "Child's Pose" on the ground. It resembled the shape of a turtle's shell, compact and secure.

As Ojii-san and Obaa-san watched in astonishment, the round shape began to shrink rapidly before their very eyes. It diminished in size until it resembled nothing more than a cylinder the shape of a diminutive 16-ounce water bottle. "Kaguya-Hime!" Ojii-san's voice pierced the air as he hastily picked up the small round object. Obaa-san, overwhelmed with emotion, could no longer contain her tears. Inside Kaguya Hime's familiar attire, Ojii-san made a bewildering discovery. Nestled on the zabuton cushion where Kaguya Hime had sat just a minute before, there lay a young, healthy bamboo shoot. There was no trace of any mystical light, just a pure and vibrant bamboo shoot.

“Was that just a dream?” Obaa-san questioned with a sob. Ojii-san replied, “It was a good, long dream that made our dream come true. And delivered a warning for the future. Obaa-san, Kaguya Hime left us a new legacy mission to save our aging earth.” Obaa-san wiped her tears with her sleeve and said, “If it is true, we have to fill our bellies first so we can plan the best for our earth. Why don’t I fix some *Takenoko Gohan* (soy sauce flavored rice with bamboo shoots) for everyone.” So she did.

Ojii-san and Obaa-san felt extremely ambitious about their new project and hopeful to collaborate with the thirty bodyguards with cool shades who would soon join their "Project Earth" task force.

After Kaguya Hime's departure, people recognized the immense value of the inventions she left behind, and the team integrated her profound insights into Project Earth. Kaguya hime's understanding of balance, respect for the environment, and the preservation of biodiversity were essential to their mission.

As thirty scientists, former bodyguards, developed the AI system, Nature's Guardian, the team allowed Kaguya Hime's wisdom to permeate its algorithms. The AI not only provided data-driven recommendations for sustainable farming practices but also emphasized the delicate equilibrium of the Earth's ecosystems. Project Earth evolved into a powerful force for change, addressing the root causes of environmental degradation. The team's understanding of the interconnectedness of all living beings grew, enabling them to implement sustainable farming practices on a larger scale. Because of Project Earth, Earth's longevity was soon on track to outlive the Moon Tribe's projections.

The team knew they were up against some major challenges. They realized that tackling these issues required a collective effort and a commitment to change. Through the team's creative social media and YouTube channels, their mission inspired individuals, communities, and governments to prioritize the preservation of our precious Earth for the sake of future generations.

In their mission to foster a deep connection with nature and inspire future generations, Ojii-san and Obaa-san integrated a school program into Project Earth. They invited children from nearby schools to participate, engaging them in interactive workshops, hands-on activities, and environmental projects in addition to the previous youth agricultural program. The school children's infectious enthusiasm and innate understanding of the Earth's interconnectedness added a vibrant energy to the project. The children served as young ambassadors of change and spread the message of sustainability within their families, communities, schools, and national conferences. Their involvement became a catalyst for positive action, igniting a collective consciousness and inspiring communities to come together for a brighter and more sustainable future.

On the moon, Kaguya Hime couldn't help but feel a sense of satisfaction as she checked the earth barometer, knowing that the Project Earth team was working tirelessly to extend the lifespan of their beloved Earth. With a heart full of happiness, she whispered affectionately, "Ojiisan, Obaa-san, Earth hit the jackpot because you chose to call it home."

Medetashi, Medetashi. Happily Ever After.

About the author

Claire E. Hallinan, MAEd's roots trace back to the traditional folktales of Japan, infusing her upbringing with enchantment. Nestled in the picturesque Pacific Northwest, she channels her passion for understanding the world, nurturing connections, and inspiring happiness into her unique storytelling style. Beyond her roles as a writer and mindfulness practitioner, Claire is a dedicated National Board Certified Teacher. Among her literary works, you'll find "Gift of Gratitude: Lessons from the Classroom," a heartfelt memoir, and "My Breath Loves Me," a Children's Picture Book radiating warmth. Explore more of Claire's creations on her Amazon Store, where her tales invite you to discover the world through her distinct lens. Follow @claire.e.hallinan on Instagram and Facebook.

www.ingramcontent.com/pod-product-compliance
Lightning Source LLC
Chambersburg PA
CBHW011142190726
48289CB00012B/3122